Trick or Treat

The Transporter platform glowed into dazzle. Then its sparkle gathered into the full figure of crewman Jackson. The hum of materialization faded. Kirk strode to the platform. "Jackson! What happened? Where are the others?"

The mouth moved as though preparing to speak. But Jackson didn't speak. The mouth twisted into a grimace—and Jackson, pitching forward, toppled to the floor.

Kneeling beside him, McCoy looked up at Kirk. He shook his head. "The man's dead, Jim."

Kirk stared down at the body. Then, horribly, the jaw dropped and the mouth opened. Out of it spoke a voice, deep, harsh, guttural. "Captain Kirk, you hear me. There is a curse on your ship. Leave this star. It is death that waits for you here . . ."

There was a moment of appalled stillness. Jackson's dead mouth still yawned open. But his lips had not moved.

STAR TREK 8

BANTAM PATHFINDER EDITIONS

A comprehensive and fully integrated series
designed to meet the expanding needs of the
young adult reading audience and the
growing demand among readers of all ages for
paperback books of high quality.

Bantam Pathfinder Editions provide the best in
fiction and nonfiction in a wide variety of
subject areas. They include novels by classic
and contemporary writers; vivid, accurate
histories and biographies; authoritative works
in the sciences; collections of short
stories, plays and poetry.

Bantam Pathfinder Editions are carefully
selected and approved. They are presented in a
new and handsome format, durably bound and
printed on specially selected high-quality paper.

STAR TREK 8
JAMES BLISH

Based on the Exciting
Television Series Created by
GENE RODDENBERRY

BANTAM PATHFINDER EDITIONS
TORONTO / NEW YORK / LONDON

A NATIONAL GENERAL COMPANY

RLI: $\dfrac{\text{VLM 7 (VLR 6–9)}}{\text{IL 7–adult}}$

STAR TREK 8
A Bantam Pathfinder edition published November 1972

Library of Congress Cataloging in Publication Data

Blish, James.
  Star trek 8.

  "Based upon the NBC-TV series created by Gene
Roddenberry."
  CONTENTS: Spock's brain.—The enemy within—Where no
man has gone before. [etc.]
  [1. Science fiction] I. Roddenberry, Gene.
II. Star trek. III. Title.
PZ7.B61915Svc   [Fic]   72-7375

Published simultaneously in the United States and Canada

Bantam Books are published by Bantam Books, Inc., a National
General company. Its trade-mark, consisting of the words "Bantam
Books" and the portrayal of a bantam, is registered in the United
States Patent Office and in other countries. Marca Registrada.
Bantam Books, Inc., 666 Fifth Avenue, New York, N.Y. 10019.

PRINTED IN THE UNITED STATES OF AMERICA

SPOCK'S BRAIN

(Lee Cronin)

The curiously elegant spaceship depicted on the *Enterprise* screen had failed to respond to any hailing frequency or to approved interstellar symbols.

Nor was its shape familiar. Scanning it, Spock said, "Design unidentified. Ion propulsion, neutron conversion of a unique technology."

Kirk said, "Magnification Ten, Mr. Chekov."

But the close-up revealed the ship as mysterious as before—a long, slender, needle-thin splinter of glow against the blackness of space.

"Well, Scotty?"

"It beats me, Captain. I've never seen anything like it. But isn't she a beauty?" He whistled in awed admiration. "And ion propulsion at that. Whoever they are, they could show us a thing or two."

"Life form readings, Mr. Spock?"

"One, sir. Humanoid or similar. Low level of activity. Life support systems functioning. Interior atmosphere conventional nitrogen oxygen." He peered more closely at his scanner. "Just a minute, Captain . . . "

"Yes, Mr. Spock?"

"Instruments indicate a transferal beam emanating from the humanoid life form."

"Directed to where?"

"To here sir—the bridge of the *Enterprise*."

People moved uneasily at their stations. Kirk spoke into the intercom. "Security guard! To the bridge!"

But even as he issued the order, a figure had begun to take shape among them. It gathered substance. A superbly beautiful woman stood in the precise center of the bridge. She was clad in a short, flowing, iridescent tunic, a human woman in all aspects save in her ex-

1

traordinary loveliness. On her arm she wore a bracelet, studded with varicolored cabochon jewels or buttons. She was smiling faintly.

Her appearance, no Transporter Room materialization, was as mysterious as the ship.

Kirk spoke. "I am Captain James T. Kirk. This is the Starship *Enterprise*."

She pressed a button on the bracelet. There was a humming sound. The bridge lights dimmed, brightened, dimmed again; and with the look of amazement still on their faces, Kirk, Spock and Scott went stiff, paralyzed. Then they crumpled to the floor. The humming sound passed out into the corridor. Again, lights flickered. Three running security guards stumbled—and fell. The humming grew louder. It moved into Sickbay where McCoy and Nurse Chapel were examining a patient. Once more, lights faded. When they brightened, McCoy, the nurse and the patient had slumped into unconsciousness.

Silence flowed in on the *Enterprise*.

Still smiling, the beautiful intruder glanced down at Kirk. She stepped over him to examine Scott's face. Then she left him to approach Spock. The smile grew in radiance as she stooped over him.

Nobody was ever to estimate accurately the duration of their tranced state. Gradually, as awareness returned to Kirk, he saw that other heads around him had recovered the power to lift themselves.

"What—where—" he asked disconnectedly.

Sulu put the question. "What happened?"

Kirk pulled himself back up into his command chair. "Status, Mr. Sulu?"

Mechanically Sulu checked his board. "No change from the last reading, sir."

"Mr. Spock?"

There was no Mr. Spock at The Vulcan's station to reply. Perplexed, Kirk looked at Scott. "The girl," Scott said dazedly, "she's gone, too."

"Yes," Kirk said, "that girl . . . "

His intercom buzzed. "Jim! Jim! Get down here to Sickbay! Right now! Jim, hurry!"

McCoy's voice had an urgency that was threaded

with horror. In Sickbay the *Enterprise*'s physician was trying to force himself to look at his own handiwork. Within its life function chamber, he had encased Spock's motionless body with a transparent bubble device. There was a small wrapping about the upper part of the cranium. Frenziedly working at his adjustment levers, he said, "Now?"

Nurse Chapel, at her small panel, nodded. She threw a switch that set lights to blinking. "It's functioning," she said, her voice weak with relief.

"Thank God."

McCoy was leaning back against the table as Kirk burst through the door.

"Bones, what in the name of—" Kirk broke off. He had seen through the transparency of the bubble. "Spock!" He glanced swiftly at the life indicator. It showed a very low level. "Well?" he demanded harshly.

It was Nurse Chapel who answered him. "I found him lying on the table when I recovered consciousness."

"Like this?"

"No," McCoy said. "Not like this."

"Well, what happened?"

"I don't know!" McCoy shouted.

"You've got him under complete life support at total levels. Was he dead?"

McCoy raised himself by a hand pushed down on the table. "It starts there," he said.

"Damn you, Bones, talk!"

"He was worse than dead."

"What do you mean?"

"Jim—" McCoy spoke pleadingly as though he were appealing for mercy from his own sense of helplessness. "Jim—his brain is gone."

"Go ahead."

"Technically, the greatest job I ever saw. Every nerve ending of the brain neatly sealed. Nothing torn, nothing ripped. No bleeding. A surgical miracle."

"Spock's brain—" Kirk said, fighting for control.

"Gone." McCoy had given up on professional composure. His voice broke. "Spock—his incredible Vulcan physique survived until I could get the support system to take over. The body lives—but it has no mind."

"The girl," Kirk said.

"What girl?"

"She took it. I don't know where—or why. But she took Spock's brain."

"Jim . . . "

"How long can you keep the body functioning?"

"Several days at the most. And I can't guarantee that."

"That's not good enough, Bones."

"If it had happened to any of us, I could say indefinitely. But Vulcan physiology limits what I can do. Spock's body is much more dependent than ours on that tremendous brain of his for life support."

"I ask you—how long, Dr. McCoy. I have to know."

Wearily, McCoy reached for the chart. "He suffered a loss of cerebral spinal fluid in the operation. Reserves are minimal. Spock's T-Negative blood supply—two total exchanges." He looked up from the chart. "Three days—no more."

Kirk moved over to the bubble. He could feel his heart cringe at the sight of the paper-white face inside it. Spock, the friend, the dear companion through a thousand hazards—Spock, the always reliable thinker, the reasonable one, the always reasonable and loyal one.

"All right, then—I've got three days."

At the naked anguish in his face, McCoy motioned the nurse to leave them alone.

"Jim, are you hoping to restore him his brain? How are you going to find it? Where are you going to look? Through the entire galaxy?"

"I'll find it."

"Even if you do find it, a brain can't be replaced with present surgical techniques."

"If it was taken, it can be put back. Obviously, there are techniques."

"I don't know them!" The cry was wrenched from McCoy.

"The thief who took it has the knowledge. I'll force it out of her! So help me, I'll get it out of her!"

It was Sulu who located the ion trail of the mystery ship.

"Look, Mr. Scott. I've got it again!"

Scott was jotting numbers down on the board in his hand. "Aye, an ion trail. It's from that ship of hers all right."

"Where does it lead, Mr. Chekov?" Kirk asked.

Chekov studied the panel at Spock's library computer. "It leads to system Sigma Draconis, sir."

"Lock on," Kirk said. "Maximum speed without losing the trail, Mr. Sulu."

"Aye, Captain. Warp six."

"Mr. Chekov, a complete readout on Sigma Draconis."

Sulu turned to Kirk. "Arrival, seven terrestrial hours, twenty-five minutes at warp six, sir."

"No mistake about the trail, Scotty?"

"No mistake, Captain."

Chekov called from Spock's station. "Coming into scanning range of the Sigma Draconis system, sir."

Alarm rang in Sulu's voice. "Captain, I've lost the trail!"

Kirk leaped from his chair. "You've lost the trail to Spock?"

"It's gone, sir. At warp six there was a sudden deactioned shift."

"No excuses, if you please," Kirk said. "All right, her trail is gone. But she was heading into this star system. She must be somewhere in it." He moved to Chekov. "Put a schematic of Sigma Draconis on the viewing screen."

The nine planets comprising the system took shape and position on the screen. "Readout, Mr. Chekov," Kirk said.

"Sun, spectral type, G–9. Three Class M planets showing sapient life. First planet rated number 5 on the industrial scale. Second Class M planet rated number 6."

"Earth equivalent, approximately 2030," Kirk estimated.

Scott broke in. "But that ship, Captain. Either it was thousands of years ahead of us—or the most incredible design fluke in history."

"Third Class M planet, Mr. Chekov?"

"Aye, sir. No signs of industrial development. Rated number 2 on the industrial scale of 20. At last report in a glacial age. Sapient life plentiful but on a most primitive level." Chekov turned around to face Kirk. "Of course, sir, in none of these cases has a detailed Federation survey been made. All the information is the result of long-range scanning and preliminary contact reports. We don't know how accurate it is."

"Understood, Mr. Chekov. There are three Class M planets, not one of which owns the capability of launching an interstellar flight. Yet one of them has obviously accomplished it."

Chekov, who had been punching up reports on the whirring computer, was too puzzled by the last one to note Kirk's irony. He compared it with what he saw on the screen before he said, "Captain, it's odd. I'm picking up high-energy generation on Planet 7."

"That's the primitive glaciated one, isn't it?"

"Yes, sir."

"Its source, Mr. Chekov?"

"It could be natural—volcanic activity, steam, any of a dozen sources, sir. But the pulsations are very regular."

"Surface readings again?"

"No signs of organized civilization. Primitive humanoids in small groups. Apparently a routine hunter-predator stage of social development."

"With very regular pulsations of generated energy?"

"I can't explain it, Captain."

Kirk turned to address all members of the bridge crew. "This time," he said, "there is no time for mistakes. We've got to pick the right planet, go there—and get what we came for. Mr. Chekov, your recommendation."

"Planet 3, sir. It's closest and the heaviest population."

Scott said, "With a technological rating of 5, it couldn't have put that ship we saw into space."

"None of these planets could," Chekov said.

"You've got to put your money where the odds are," Scott retorted. "Captain, my guess is Planet 4. Technologically it's ahead of 3."

"Yes," Kirk said. "But ion propulsion is beyond even our technology. Can you really credit theirs with its development?"

Uhura spoke up. "And what would they want with Mr. Spock's brain?"

"What?" Kirk said.

"I said what would they want with Mr. Spock's brain? What use could they make of it? Why should they want it?"

Kirk stared at her. "A very interesting question, Lieutenant. Why indeed should they want it? Planet 7. It's glaciated, you say, Mr. Chekov?"

"Yes, sir. For several thousand years at least. Only the tropical zone is ice-free—and that would be bitterly cold. Humanoids exist on it; but only under very trying conditions."

"But the energy, Mr. Chekov. It's there."

"Yes, sir. It doesn't make sense—but it's there."

Kirk sat back in his chair. Three days—and Spock's body would be a dead one. Choice. Choice again. Decision again—command decision. He made it.

"I'm taking a landing party down to Planet 7," he said.

Scott stirred uncomfortably.

"Well, Mr. Scott?"

"Nothing, sir."

"Very well. We'll transport down immediately."

Kirk had seen some bleak landscapes in his time; but this one, he thought, would take the cake at any galactic fair.

What vegetation there was scarcely deserved the name, sparse as it was, brown, crackling under the feet with hardened frost. No green, just rocks, black under the sprinkling of snow that clung to their harsh crags, their crannies. A constant icy wind blew. He shivered, hoping that the rest of his party—McCoy, Scott, Chekov and two security guards—were as grateful as he was for their lightweight, thermal cold-weather clothing.

"Readings, Mr. Scott." His warm breath congealed in a mist as he spoke.

"Scattered life forms, widely spaced. Humanoid all right. On the large side."

"Watch out for them. They are primitives. Readout, please, Mr. Chekov."

Chekov unslung his tricorder, and went to work on the rocky plateau where they had materialized. His explorations acquired a witness. Above him was an escarpment, broken by a gulch, sheltered by an over-hang of stunted scrub. A fur-clad figure, armed with a crude knobbed club, had scrambled through the gulch; and was lying now, belly-flat, at the edge of the cliff to peer through the overhang at what went on below.

Chekov returned to his party. "No structures, Captain. No surface consumption of energy or generation of it. Atmosphere OK. Temperature—say a high maximum of forty. Livable."

"If you've got a thick skin," McCoy said.

The figure on the cliff had been joined by several other skin-clad creatures, their faces hidden by parkalike hoods. They moved, gathering, from rock to rock as though closing in. Most carried the heavy clubs. One bore a spear.

"Captain!" Chekov cried. "There's someone—something up there. There—up on that cliff . . ."

"Phasers on stun," Kirk ordered. "Fire only on my signal."

Chekov looked up again from his tricorder. "I register six of them, sir. Humanoids. Big."

"Remember, I want one of them conscious," Kirk said.

As he spoke, a huge man, savagely bearded, rose up on the cliff; and swinging his club in an arc over his head, hurled it downward. It struck a security guard a glancing blow. He yelled in surprise and alarm. The alarm in the yell brought the other five to their feet.

They all clambered up to shower the *Enterprise* with rocks and clubs.

Aiming his phaser at one of them, Kirk fired. The man fell and rolled down the cliff's slope, stunned. Shouting to each other, the rest disappeared.

The prisoner belonged to a hardleaded lot. Consciousness returned to him with astonishing swiftness. He struggled to rise, but Scott seized him with a judo hold that suggested the reprisal of pain for struggle. The man (and he was a man) subsided. He looked up at Kirk, terror in his eyes. Extending his empty hands in a gesture of friendship, Kirk said, "We mean you no harm. We are not enemies. We want to be your friends."

The terror in the eyes abated slightly. Kirk spoke again. "We will not hurt you. We only want to talk to you. Let him go, Mr. Scott."

"Captain, he could twist your head off."

"Let him go," Kirk repeated.

The man said, "You are not The Others?"

"No," Kirk said. "We are not The Others. We come from a far place."

"You are small like The Others. I could break you in two."

"But you won't," Kirk said. "We are men. Like you. Why did you attack us?"

"When The Others come, we fight. We thought you were The Others."

"Who are The Others?"

"They are the givers of pain and delight."

"Do they live here with you?"

"They come."

"Where do you see them when they come?"

The man spread his arms wide. "Everywhere. On the hunt, when we eat, at the time of sleep."

"The Others—where do they come from?"

Kirk got a heavy stare. "Do they come from the sky?" he asked.

"They are here. You will see. They will come for you. They come for all like us."

"Jim, ask him about women," McCoy said. He spoke

to the man himself. "Do The Others come for your women, too?"

"Women?"

"The females of our kind," Kirk said.

The man shrugged. "Your words say nothing."

Kirk tried again. "We are looking for a—lost friend."

"If he is here, The Others have him."

"Will you take us where we can find The Others?"

"No one wants to find The Others."

"We do. Take us to them and we will let you go."

"Captain!" Chekov, his tricorder switched to full power, was pointing excitedly to the ground. "Right where we're standing, there's a foundation below the surface! And masonry debris! There are registrations all over the place!"

"Buildings?"

"Unquestionably, sir. Immensely old and completely buried. I don't know how our sensors misread them."

"Then somewhere below us is where The Others live," Kirk said. "Mr. Scott, check it out."

Scott and a guard were moving away when a hoarse cry came from the fur-clad man. "Don't go!" he screamed. "Don't go!"

Chekov and McCoy tried to calm him. He refused calm. He pulled madly out of their hold, shrieking with terror. "Release him," Kirk said. They obeyed.

"Don't go!" The last warning was almost a sob. Then he was gone, frantically hauling himself back up the cliff. Chekov said, "What have these Others done to cause such fear?"

"We may know soon enough," was McCoy's sober reply.

"Bones, what was it he said The Others give? It was 'pain and delight,' wasn't it?"

"A peculiar mixture, Jim."

"Everything's peculiar," Kirk said. "A dead and buried city on a planet in the glacial age . . ."

"And a man," said Chekov, "who doesn't know the meaning of the word 'women.' "

"There's a thread somewhere that ties it all together," Kirk said thoughtfully. "Right now I wish I had Spock here to find it for me. No offense, Mr. Chekov."

Chekov said fervently, "I wish it, too, sir."

"It's beginning to look as though your hunch was right, Jim. If there was a city here, maybe millions of years ago . . . "

Kirk nodded. "Then it could have developed a science capable of building that ship we saw."

"Captain, over here, sir." Scott and a security guard were standing near a spur of rock jutting out from the cliff. Under it was an opening, large enough to make entrance accessible to even one of the huge, shaggy, fur-clad men. It led into a cave. Or a room. Or something else. "I've looked inside," Scott said. "There's food in there, Captain."

"Food?"

"And a whole pile of other stuff. Some kind of cache. You'd better look, sir."

The place was about twelve feet square. It should have been dark. It wasn't. It was quite light enough to see the food, mounds of it, laid out neatly along one wall. Furs were stacked against another along with clubs, metal knives, tools, hatchets. "A storehouse," McCoy said, "for our muscular friends."

"I don't think so, Bones."

Kirk picked up a crude metal ax. "Forged," he said, "tempered. Our savage brothers did not make this." He returned to the cave's entrance to run his fingers along its edges. They were smooth. He came slowly back to examine the place more closely. Then he saw it—a light which alternately glowed and faded. It came from a small cell set into the wall behind the piled food. He waited. The light went into glow—and shot a beam across the food to a cell in the opposite wall.

"Scotty, Bones," he called. As they approached him, he barred their forward movement with an arm. The light glowed—and he gestured toward the beam. "What do you think?"

"It could be a warning device to keep those beast boys away from the food," Scott said.

"You think that beam could kill?" McCoy asked him.

"It very well might."

"How about this?" Kirk looked thoughtful. "The food is a lure to bring those primitive men into this place."

"In that case, Captain, the beam might be serving as a signal of their arrival."

"And this cave," Kirk said, "could be a trap."

"It could trap us, too, then, Captain," Chekov said nervously.

"Yes," Kirk said. "So you and the security team will remain at the entrance. We will maintain contact with you. If you don't hear from us within five hours, you will return to the *Enterprise* and contact Starfleet Command. Understood?"

"Yes, sir."

"Then return to the entrance."

"Yes, sir."

At Kirk's nod, Scott and McCoy checked their communicators. McCoy slung his tricorder over his shoulder. Then all three stepped over the beam. Kirk turned. Behind them metal doors had dropped over the cave's entrance.

"Phasers on stun," he said.

A loud hum broke the silence. Its pitch increased to a whine—and the whole cave moved bodily under their feet, descending as a descending elevator descends. It continued its smooth downward plunge; and Scott, checking his tricorder, said, "Captain, that power we picked up before—we're getting closer to it."

"A lot of power?" Kirk asked.

"Enough to push this planet out of orbit."

The whining noise was diminishing. "Natural or artificial, Mr. Scott?"

"Artificial, I'd say, sir."

"And the source?"

"Either a nuclear pile a hundred miles wide or . . ."

"Or what, Mr. Scott?"

"Ion power."

Kirk smiled thinly. Ion power—it had stolen Spock. He had to fight against an uprush of rage. Then he decided to let it happen to him. He'd use it to sharpen every sense he had. He succeeded. The door of the

cave-elevator had been fitted so deftly into it that he
alone spotted it before it slid silently open. A young
girl was facing them. Kirk's eyes looked for and found
the button-studded bracelet on her arm. Her face had
tightened in surprise and fear. But before she could
stab at her bracelet, Kirk fired his phaser. She fell.

Scott stood guard while Kirk removed the bracelet.
"Is she all right, Bones?" he asked as McCoy rose from
her stunned body.

"I'll have her talking in a minute—if she talks."

The pretty eyelids opened. At once her right hand
went to her left arm. Kirk dangled the bracelet in her
face. "We've had enough of that trick," he said.

She was instantly on her feet to make a grab for the
bracelet. As McCoy's firm hold convinced her of her
helplessness, she said, "You do not belong here. You
are not morg."

Kirk ignored that. "Take us to the one in charge," he
said. "We must talk to him."

"Him? What is him?" said the girl. "I am Luma and
I know no him."

"Who is in charge here?" Kirk's patience was slipping. "Where is the brain? Where was it taken? Do you
understand me?"

"You do not belong here. You are not morg or
eymorg. I know nothing about a brain."

"I'll say you don't!" Kirk said. "I have no time for
stupid lies!"

"Jim—she's not lying. I've checked her. She really
doesn't know." McCoy reslung his tricorder over his
shoulder; and the girl seized her moment to make a
wild dash for a door at the end of the corridor. Kirk
caught her just as she reached it, but she had managed
to press a photo cell built into the door jamb. Spinning
her around, he barred her way through it.

"What is this place?" he demanded.

"This place is here."

"Who are you?"

"I say before I am Luma. I am eymorg. You are not
eymorg. You are not morg. What you are I do not
understand."

"Well," Kirk said, "they certainly seem to be in bad need of brains around here. Watch her, Scotty."

"You'll get nothing out of that one, Captain. She's got the mind of a child."

"Then she's got a sister who isn't retarded!" Kirk said. "One that she can take us to! I've had all I'm taking of these pleas of ignorance!"

He flipped the dial on his communicator. "Captain Kirk to Chekov—Kirk to Chekov. Come in, Mr. Chekov!"

There was no response. He altered the dial adjustment and tried again. "Kirk to Chekov. Come in, Mr. Chekov . . ."

"Fascinating. Activity without end. But with no volition—fascinating."

Kirk froze. A chill shook him from head to feet. It was Spock's voice, familiar, loved, speaking very slowly.

"Fascinat—" Kirk shouted into the communicator. "Spock! Spock! Is that you?"

"Captain? Captain Kirk?"

"Yes, Spock! Yes!"

"It's good to hear a voice, especially yours."

Wordless, his hands shaking, Kirk handed his communicator to McCoy. Joy in his voice, McCoy cried, "Where are you, Spock? We're coming to get you!"

"Is that you, Dr. McCoy? Are you with the Captain?"

"Where else would I be?" In his turn McCoy silently passed the communicator to Scott.

"Where are you, Mr. Spock?"

"Engineer Scott, too? Unfortunately, I do not know where I am."

Kirk grabbed the communicator. "We'll get to you, Spock. It won't be long. Hold on."

"Good. Captain. It seems most unlikely that I will be able to get to you."

McCoy spoke again. "If you don't know where you are, do you know what they're doing with you? That could help us."

"Sorry, Doctor. I have not been able to achieve any insight into that."

"They are using you for something," insisted McCoy.

"Perhaps you are right. At the moment I do not feel useful. Functional in some ways—but not useful."

"Spock," Kirk said, "keep concentrating. The use they are making of you will determine where they have you. Keep concentrating on the use they are making of you—and we'll get to you."

The door beside them slid open. Two of the shaggy men came through it. Metal bands encircled their brows. They were welded into other bands that passed over their heads and down to cup their chins. Behind them stood the beautiful passenger of the ion-propelled spaceship.

She motioned the men toward Kirk, McCoy and Scott. They didn't move. She pushed a red stud on her bracelet. The banded men writhed in torment. In a paroxysm of mixed pain and frustrated fury, they charged the *Enterprise* party. McCoy, caught off guard, felt a rib crack under the pressure of two massively muscular arms. Kirk had pulled free of his attacker's grip. He bent his back under the next maddened assault and his man slid over it into a somersault. He found his phaser, fired it—and the morg, the man, lay still. Then he felled Scott's adversary with a karate blow.

This time the beautiful lady chose to depress a yellow button on her bracelet. Kirk's phaser dropped from his hand as unconsciousness flooded over him. Like the two morgs, like Scott and McCoy, he lay still.

The five male bodies, helplessly stretched at her feet, pleased the lady. When the girl Luma joined her, the spectacle pleased her, too.

It was a woman's world under the planet's surface.

In its Council Chamber, women, all physically attractive, sat at a T-shaped table. As the still triumphantly smiling lady took her place at its head, they rose, bowed and caroled, "Honor to Kara the Leader!" Beside each woman knelt a man, sleek, well fed, docile as a eunuch. Occasionally a woman stroked a man as one pats a well-housebroken pet.

At Kara's signal a door opened. Two of the muscular kitten-men pushed Kirk, McCoy and Scott into the room and up to the head of the table. The metal bands had now been fixed to their heads. Their masculinity caused a stir among the women; but it was the response, not of adult women, but of children on their first visit to a zoo.

Scott was the first to recognize Kara. "She's the one who came to the *Enterprise*," he whispered to Kirk.

Kirk nodded. "It's the smile I remember," he said.

She spoke. "You have a thing to say?" she asked pleasantly.

"Just one thing," Kirk said. "What have you done with the brain of my First Officer?"

"We do not know your First Officer."

"His brain," Kirk said. "You have Spock's brain."

Something registered in what passed for Kara's brain. "Ah, yes! Brain! You spoke to Luma also of brain. We do not understand."

They *are* retardates, Kirk thought. Getting through to whatever gray matter existed in that beautiful head was going to be tough. Temper, temper! he said to himself. Speaking slowly, very distinctly, "You were on my Starship," he said. "You were there to take Spock's brain. What's more, you took it. So what's this talk of not understanding what I mean by brain?"

"We do not know these things you speak of. We are only here below and here above. This is our place. You are not a morg. You are stranger."

Kirk's temper refused to heed his exhortation. "You came to my ship . . ."

McCoy put a restraining hand on his arm. "Jim, she may not remember. Or even really know. Dissociation may be complete. One thing is sure. She never performed that operation."

"If it required intelligence, she certainly didn't," Kirk said.

Kara pointed to Luma. "You hurt her. It is not permitted again to hurt anyone."

"We are sorry," Kirk said. "We did not wish to hurt."

"You wish to return to your home? You may go."

Kirk rallied all the charm he'd occasionally been accused of possessing. "We wish to stay here with you.

We wish to learn from you. And tell you about us. Then we will not be stranger."

The women were delighted. They smiled and nodded at each other. McCoy decided to toss his charm into the pot. "Above," he said, "it is cold, harsh. Below here with you, it is warm. Perhaps it is your beauty that freshens the air."

They liked that, too. They liked it so much that Scott was encouraged to say, "There is no sun. Yet there is light—the light of your loveliness."

Kirk had lost his last shred of patience. "I want to meet those in charge," he said.

"In charge?" echoed Kara.

She looked so puzzled that he added, "The leader of your people."

"Leader? I am Leader. There is no other."

Dumbfounded, Scott said, "Who runs your machines?"

Kirk drew a deep breath. "This is a complex place," he said. "Who controls it?"

"Control?" she said. "Controller?"

The shocked look on her face told him the word had meaning for her. He tried to subdue his rising excitement. "Controller! Yes! That is right. We would like to meet—to see your controller!"

Kara's fury was as abrupt as it was intense. "It is not permitted! Never! Controller is apart, alone! We serve Controller! No other is permitted near!"

"We intend no harm," Kirk said hastily.

But he had exploded a volcano. "You have come to destroy us!" Kara screamed. The women around her, infected by her panic, twittered like birds at the approach of a snake. They all rose, their fingers reaching for their bracelets. Appalled, Kirk cried, "No! No! We do not come to destroy you! We are not destroyers!" McCoy came to stand beside him. He put all the reassurance at his disposal into his voice. "All we want," he said, "is to talk to somebody about Spock's brain."

"Brain! And again, brain! What is brain? It is Controller, is it not?"

McCoy said, "Well, yes. In a way it is. The human brain controls the individual's functions." He was beginning to suspect the significance of the hysteria. He looked at Kirk. "And the controlling power of the Vulcan brain, Jim, is extraordinarily powerful."

Scott, too, had realized that Kara identified the word "brain" with controlling power. "Is it possible they are using Spock's brain to—" He didn't complete the sentence.

"The fact that it is a Vulcan brain makes it possible," McCoy said.

Kirk suddenly flung himself to his knees. "Great Leader! We have come from a far place to learn from your Controller . . . "

"You lie! You have come to take the Controller! You have said this!"

Still on his knees, Kirk said, "He is our friend. We beg you to take us to him."

But the fright in the women's faces had increased. One began to sob. Kara stood up. "Quiet! There is no need to fear. We know they can be prevented." The women refused consolation. As though the very sight of the *Enterprise* men filled them with horror, they pushed their benches back and fled the Council Chamber.

Kirk made a leap for Kara. "You must take us to him!" he shouted.

She touched the red stud on her bracelet. The bands cupping their heads were suddenly clawed with fiery spindles. They stabbed their temples with an excruciating agony that obliterated thought, the memory of Spock, of the *Enterprise*, the world itself. The torture widened, spread to their throats, their chests, devouring their breath. Choking, Kirk tore at the band and collapsed. Beside him, McCoy and Scott had lost consciousness.

"I must learn what to do!" Kara cried. "Keep them here!"

Her two servant morgs hesitated. She moved a finger toward her bracelet. The gesture was sufficient. They lumbered over to the slumped bodies to take up guard positions on either side of them.

The pain had ceased. Kirk opened his eyes to see McCoy stir feebly. "Are you all right, Bones?" McCoy nodded, his eyes bloodshot. "I—I wouldn't have believed the human body could have survived such pain," he whispered. Revived, Scott was pulling at his headband. "They're attached to us by a magnetic lock of some kind."

"No wonder the morgs are so obedient," Kirk said. He struggled back to his feet. "What beats me is how this place is kept functioning. What keeps the air pure and the temperature equable?"

"It's clearly not the men," McCoy said. "They live on the frozen surface like beasts. So it must be the women. They live down here with all the comforts of an advanced society."

"Not one of those women could have set up the complex that keeps the place going," Scott said. "That would call on engineering genius. There is no sign of genius in these females."

"They're smart enough to have evolved these headbands," Kirk said. "What a way to maintain control over men!"

" 'Pain and delight,' " McCoy quoted. "I'm sure you've noticed the delight aspect in these surroundings, Jim."

"Yes. Beauty, sex, warmth, food—and all of them under the command of the women."

"And how does Spock's brain fit into this woman-commanded underground?" Scott asked.

Kirk didn't answer. The guard morgs had left them to go and stand at a corner table. On it, neatly arranged, were their tricorders and communicators. Only their phasers were missing. "Bones," Kirk said, "do you see what I see over there?"

"The equipment is only there, Jim, because the women don't understand its use."

"Gentlemen," Kirk said, "wouldn't you say that science holds the answer to the problem of recovering our equipment?"

"Aye," Scott said. "Let's go, Captain!"

They went for the morgs. Kirk gripped the jaw of one in a hard press. There was a bellow of pain. Terrified that it had been heard, the other morg looked apprehensively toward the door. Then he made a jump for Scott. Both guards were paragons of muscular strength; but their long training in docility had destroyed their ability to use it effectively. Kirk downed his Goliath with a jab to the throat. Scott's rabbit punch disposed of the other rabbit. Scientific fighting indeed held the answer to their problem. Within forty seconds the two guards were out for the count.

Kirk hastily adjusted the high-power dial on his communicator. "Spock! Spock! This channel reached you. Come in, Spock! Kirk here."

"Yes, Captain." It was Spock's voice. "I am also here. But I begin to feel extended almost to infinity. Have you returned to the *Enterprise?*"

"No! We were just temporarily out of—communication."

"You have not been seriously injured, I trust?"

"No! Spock, have you discovered what use you are being put to? Is it medical or . . . "

"I am not sure, sir. I seem to have a body that stretches into endlessness."

"Body?" Scott blurted. "You have no body!"

"No body? But then what am I?"

"You are a disembodied brain," McCoy said.

"Really? Fascinating. That could explain much. My medulla oblongata is apparently directing my breathing, pumping my blood and maintaining a normal physiological temperature."

"Spock," McCoy said, "keeping a detached brain alive is a medical miracle. But keeping it functioning, that's impossible."

"I would agree with you, Doctor, if it were not the present fact. It seems incontrovertible that my brain *is* functioning, does it not?"

"It does, Spock, I must admit. And gladly, for once."

"How was the operation accomplished?"

"We don't know."

"Then why are you endangering your lives by coming here?"

"We've come to take you back," Kirk said.

"Back where? To my body?"

"Yes, Spock."

"Thoughtful, Captain. But probably impractical. My body . . . "

McCoy took the communicator. "Don't you think I had the sense to slap it into our life support chamber?"

"Of course. But I do not believe you own the skill or knowledge to replace a brain, Doctor. That skill does not yet exist in the galaxy."

Kirk removed the communicator from McCoy. "The skill that removed the brain exists right here. The skill to replace it may exist here, too."

"Captain, how much time has elapsed since my brain was removed?"

"Forty-eight hours."

"Sir, Dr. McCoy must have told you that seventy-two hours is the maximum my body can be . . . "

"I know, Spock. That leaves us fourteen hours."

"It seems all too brief a time to develop the required skill, Captain."

"Very brief. One question, Spock. Pain-causing bands have been fixed to our heads. Do you know how to get us free of them? They have to come off."

"I shall consider it, sir," the voice said.

"Give it top priority. And stay with us, Spock. Kirk out."

They moved cautiously out of the Council Chamber into the corridor. It was empty. Kirk spoke soberly. "As the lady said, gentlemen, we are not morg. We are disciplined men, intelligent, committed to a purpose. We will remain committed to it in spite of any pain inflicted upon us."

His communicator crackled. "I have the answer for you, Captain. Your pain bands are manually controlled. A blue button on a bracelet releases them. That doesn't make much sense but . . . "

"Oh yes, it does," Kirk said. "Thank you, Spock."

A blue button. He must remember. They were extremely color-prone in this place. The ornamented door at the end of the corridor blazed with color like a stained-glass window. It seemed to possess other qualities. Though they were approaching it slowly, McCoy's tricorder had begun to buzz loudly. With every careful step they took, the volume increased in intensity until

McCoy said, "I'm tuning out. The power is too great for the tricorder."

"Spock," Kirk said into his communicator, "do you know whether you are close to the power source?"

"I can't tell that. But you, Captain, are very close to it."

It was a credible statement. Near now to the elaborate door, they could see that its colored bosses were radiating a dazzling luminescence. They pushed it open to be faced by a wall banked with shining instrumentation. The room might have been the laboratory of magicians versed in the mysteries of some arcane technology. Another wall was a gigantic control board, topped by a helmetlike device. Near it a large black box set on a metallic pedestal was massed with photoelectric cells, all adjusted to correspond to similar cells on the control board. They flashed together in a constant interchange of energy.

Kara, her body taut, was standing before the black box, her back to them.

She heard them, despite their care. She whirled, her hand instantly touching her bracelet. The agony seared them, ripping a scream from Scott. They stumbled on, their legs rubber, their chests on fire. Kirk reached her, tore her hand from her bracelet and wrenched it off her arm. The blue button. He pressed it—and their headbands snapped. Kara gave a wild cry.

It echoed and re-echoed endlessly. Then they saw what stretched beyond the room—a vast machinery that extended for hundreds of underground miles, utterly alien, gleaming, no element in its panels and coils familiar. Awed into silence, Scott finally found his voice. "Captain, it is the ultimate. I think that is an air recirculation unit—but I'm not sure. I'm not even sure this is a hydroponic regulator. It all seems to have been contrived for life support—but it's a work of genius that is beyond me."

Kirk had his eyes on the black box. It glittered under the light rays that streamed to it from all sections of the great control board. How he knew what he knew he didn't know. He walked up to it. "Spock," he said, "you are in a black box tied with light rays to a complex control panel."

The voice sounded very close. "Incredible!" it said.

"Spock, you said you were breathing, pumping blood, maintaining temperature. Are you also recirculating air, running heating systems, purifying water?"

"Indeed, Captain, that is exactly what I'm doing."

Kara had broken free of McCoy's grip. Frenzied, she rushed at Kirk, trying to push him away from the box. He seized her; and she sagged, screaming, "We will die! You must not take the Controller! We will die! The Controller is young, powerful—perfect!"

"Extremely flattering," said the black box.

She flung herself to the floor, groping for Kirk's knees. "Leave him with us! He will give life to us for ten thousand years!"

"You will find another Controller," Kirk said.

She was sobbing. "There exists no other in the world. The old one is finished. Our new one must stay with us!"

Spock's voice spoke. "Captain, there seem to be rather complex problems. My brain is maintaining life for a large population. Remove it—and the life support systems it supports come to a stop."

McCoy looked somber. "Jim, here his brain is alive. If you remove it from the connections that are feeding it now to turn it over to me, it may die."

"That is the risk," Spock said. "Captain, much as I long for reunion with you and the *Enterprise*, the prospect of betraying such a dependent society is disturbing to a conscience like mine."

"Rubbish!" said Kirk. "Pure rationalization. It's always provoked by a weeping woman. She took your brain out—and she can put it back!" He shook Kara roughly. "How did you remove the brain?"

"I do not know."

"She couldn't know, Jim. Her mental faculties are almost atrophied. The Controller has done all her thinking for her."

"*She took it out!*" Kirk shouted. He shook Kara again. "*How did you do it?*"

"It was—the old knowledge," she whimpered.

"How did you get the knowledge?"

"I put—the teacher on my head."

"What teacher?"

She pointed to the helmetlike device. "What did you do with it?" Kirk demanded. "Show us!"

She shrieked in horror. "It is forbidden! The ancients forbade it. Only on the command of the ancients can I know."

"*Show us,*" Kirk said.

Hysterical tears swelling her face, Kara got to her feet, went to the control board and reached for the helmet. Lifting it reverently down, she slowly lowered it over her head. Over the sobs that convulsed her, Spock's voice said, "If I may explain, Captain. She referred to the taped storehouse of knowledge accumulated by the builders of this place. It is a most impressive store. I scan it. The tapes are circuited to lead into the helmet. When placed over the head of the priestess leader, their information penetrates her mind. It is used rarely—and only when predetermined by the builders."

It was another credible statement. Under the helmet, Kara's face had changed. It had been wiped clean of her infantile hysteria. Into her eyes had come a searching look, the alertness of active thinking. Even her voice had taken on the vibrancy of intelligence. She spoke with clipped clarity. "That explanation is essentially correct. However, the Controller gives no credit to me. I deserve it. I provide the means by which the knowledge is used. Without me, Captain of the *Enterprise* . . . "

This Kara was a woman to take into account. McCoy acknowledged the difference. "That is true. Without you the miracle that has kept Spock's brain alive could not have occurred."

She bowed with dignity. "Thank you, Doctor."

Kirk said, "We all appreciate your contribution."

"Good," she said. "Then you will also appreciate your own contribution—*this* . . . "

A phaser was in her hand.

"Captain!" Scott cried. "It's on the kill mark!"

"So it is," she said. "And that is the knowledge *you* have given to me—how to kill!"

Kirk was the first to rally. "You knew how to kill before we came. You are killing Spock by keeping his brain."

She laughed. "The Controller die? He will live ten thousand years!"

"But Spock will be dead. Even now his body is dying. Soon it will be too late to restore him life."

"No. Only the vessel that once contained the Controller will be dead."

"But the body and the brain comprise a being," Kirk said.

The phaser didn't waver in its aim. Above it, her eyes were very bright. "Spare me such opinions. You will stay here quietly with me until the vessel is dead. Then we shall say good-bye and you can return to your ship."

"Your ancients are using you to murder," Kirk said.

She smiled. "Their commandment is being obeyed."

"Commandments older than your ancients' forbid murder," Kirk said.

She was shaken by the cold intensity of his voice. "Why do you not understand? My people need their Controller more then you need your friend."

A sense of the righteousness of his wrath swept over Kirk like a great wave. For the first time in his life he understood the meaning of "towering" rage. It seemed to lift him up to a great height. He extended a finger at her. "No one may take the life of another. Not for any purpose. It is not allowed."

He stepped forward. The phaser lifted. Then it drooped. Behind her, Scott quietly reached an arm over her shoulder—and took the phaser. Her eyes filled with silent tears.

"The commandment," she whispered, "should be fulfilled."

"You will help us," Kirk said. "How long does the knowledge last?"

"Three kyras," she said.

"You will restore what you stole," Kirk said.

"And betray my people? No."

"Jim—if the helmet worked for her, it might work for me." McCoy moved to Kara, lifted the helmet from her head—and Spock's voice spoke. "The configurations of her brain are alien, Doctor. It could burn your brain right out."

"I am a surgeon. If I can learn these techniques, I might retain them."

"Bones, how long can we keep the brain functioning once we remove it from its current environment?"

"Five or six hours."

"When it's tied to our life support system, will it give us any more time?"

"A few more hours."

Spock's voice said, "I cannot allow such risk to the Doctor."

McCoy handed the helmet to Kirk. He went to the box. "Spock, Spock, didn't you hear me? I may retain the memory of these techniques to pass on to the world! Isn't that worth the risk to me? *You* would take such a risk! Would you deny the same right to me?"

Kirk said, "Take the helmet, Bones. Put it on."

Slowly McCoy lowered the device over his head. From the black box words came. "Mr. Scott, go to the left lower quarter of the control board . . ."

"Yes, sir.

"Have you located a small lever in that sector?"

"Yes, Mr. Spock."

"Depress it exactly two notches and force it sharply into the slit on the right."

A low humming sounded. As power moved from the control board into the helmet's circuitry, McCoy's hand went to his throat. His body and his face seemed to disconnect. His face glowed as though he'd been struck with some final illumination, but his body convulsed in torture. Then he blacked out and keeled over. Scott hastily pulled the lever back into its original position, then he and Kirk rushed to McCoy and gently lifted the helmet from his head. Kirk sat down, holding the unconscious body—and McCoy's eyes opened.

The vagueness in them disappeared. They began to brighten, first in wonder, then in exaltation. He gave a great shout of pure joy. "Of course—of course—a child could do it. A little child could do it!"

"Good luck to you, Dr. McCoy," said the black box.

In the *Enterprise*'s Sickbay, the operating room had been prepared.

Spock lay on its sheet-shrouded table, a shield screening the upper section of his head. Behind the shield, Nurse Chapel, a look of amazement on her face, was concentrated on every move made by the surgical instruments in McCoy's rubber-gloved hands. He was working with an authority she'd never seen before in a human surgeon. She took the time to wish that Kirk and Scott could see what she was privileged to see. But they, with Kara, had been placed behind a grille.

She went to the grille to whisper to Kirk. "Captain, don't worry. It's not to be believed—the way he's fusing ganglia, nerve endings, even individual nerves almost too small to see—and as if he'd been doing it all his life."

"How much longer?" Kirk said.

"I can't tell, sir. He's going so much faster than is humanly possible."

"Time is important," he said. "There's no way of knowing how long we can count on this increased surgical knowledge to last."

Kara suddenly sobbed. Kirk placed an arm about her shoulder. "What is it?" he said.

"You will have him back. But we are destroyed."

He led her out into the corridor. "No," he said, "you are not destroyed. You'll have no Controller and that will be fine. You will have to come up from below and live on the surface."

"We will die in the cold."

"No, you won't. We will help you until you can help yourselves. You will build houses. You'll learn to keep warm by working to keep warm. You'll learn how to be women instead of hothouse plants."

"Captain Kirk!"

Nurse Chapel was at the Sickbay door. "You'd better come quickly, sir!"

McCoy had stopped working. He had backed away from the operating table. He looked sick. "I—can't. I—I can't . . . "

"He's forgetting, Captain," said Nurse Chapel.

"Bones!" Kirk called through the grille.

McCoy stumbled toward him. "All the ganglia—the nerves—a million of them—what am I supposed to do with them? The thalamus—the pallium . . . "

"Bones! You can't stop now!"

Nurse Chapel, her eyes on the life support indicator, said, "Doctor—the cerebral spinal fluid is almost exhausted."

McCoy groaned. "But—I don't know what to do. It's gone—I don't remember—no one can replace a brain!"

"But you could, Bones! It was child's play just a short while ago!"

"It's all gone, Jim. He's going to die—and I can't stop it!"

"Dr. McCoy."

Half-strangled, choked, it was nevertheless Spock's voice. They stared at the body on the sheeted table. McCoy was astounded into asking, "Spock, did you speak? How did you speak?"

"If you will finish connecting my vocal cords, I may be able to help."

McCoy rushed behind the shield. He chose an instrument. Then he discarded it, picked up another one and gave a brisk order to Nurse Chapel. Spock suddenly coughed. The voice came a little stronger. "Good. One thing at a time. Now, Doctor, try the sonic separator. No discouragement . . . "

"No, Spock—it's been like trying to thread a needle with a sledgehammer."

"No discouragement," Spock repeated. "I already have feeling, sensation. Now stimulate the nerve endings and observe the reactions. I shall tell you when the probe is correct. When I tell you, seal the endings with the trilaser connector."

Kirk spoke to McCoy. "Well?"

His answer came in a slight hum from behind the shield. Through the grille, he could see Spock's arms move, moving normally, up and down, bending normally at the elbow.

"Very good," Spock said. "Now, Doctor, please

move to reconnect the major blood vessels. Begin with the carotid artery."

His face drawn with strain, McCoy glanced over at Kirk. "Even if this works," he said, "I'll never live it down—this confounded Vulcan telling me how to operate!"

Relief swamped Kirk. They were back at the old bickering. McCoy had paused to allow Nurse Chapel to wipe the sweat from his forehead. He returned to work and Spock said, "They are sealed, Doctor."

"Are they, Bones?"

McCoy raised his head. "How do I know? He knows. I've probably made a thousand mistakes— sealing individual nerve endings, joining ganglia. The fluid balance is right but—I don't know."

Nurse Chapel was wiping his forehead again when Spock's eyelids flickered. The eyes opened. Spock lifted his head and his eyebrows went up into the arch McCoy thought never to see again. He shouted, "Jim!"

Kirk strode behind the shield. Spock was sitting up. "Gentlemen," he said, "it is a pleasure to see you again."

"Spock—Spock," Kirk said—and swallowed. "How do you feel?"

"On the whole, I believe I am quite fit, sir."

He started to get off the table. "For the Lord's sake, take it easy!" Kirk yelled.

Spock winced under a twinge of pain. "Perhaps you are right, Captain. I seem to have something of a headache. Perhaps I had better close my eyes."

"You are going to sleep and sleep and sleep," Kirk said.

Spock sleepily closed his eyes and immediately opened them in obvious surprise. "The eyelids work," he said. "Fascinating! It would seem, Doctor, that few of your connections were made in error."

"I performed a miracle of surgery on you to get you back into one piece," McCoy said.

"Doctor, I regret that I was unable to provide you with a blueprint."

McCoy turned to Kirk. "What I'll never know is why I reconnected his mouth to his brain."

Scott came out of the bridge elevator.

"Our technical aid teams have been beamed down to Planet 7, Captain."

"First reports, Mr. Scott?"

Scott rubbed his chin. "Well, sir, restoring friendly relations between its males and females won't be easy. Neither sex trusts the other one."

"How very human," commented Spock.

"And very cold," McCoy put in. "Especially the women. However, the aid parties have provided the ladies with a tool for procuring food, furs and fuel from the men."

"Oh?" Kirk turned from one to the other. "Money?"

"No, sir," Scott said. "Perfume."

"I'm not given to predictions, gentlemen, but I'll venture one now," Kirk told them. "The sexual conflict on Planet 7 will be a short one."

"I fail to see what facts you base your prediction on, Captain," Spock said.

"On long, cold winter nights, Mr. Spock—on the fact that cuddling is so much warmer than wood fires."

"Cuddling, sir?"

"A human predilection, Spock," McCoy said. "We don't expect you to know about it."

"Of course not, Doctor. It is a well-known fact that we Vulcans propagate our race by mail." He grinned.

"Spock!" McCoy shouted. "You smiled! No, by George, you positively grinned!"

"Another tribute to your surgery, Doctor. I was endeavoring to sneeze."

"Well, of all the ungrateful patients I—" McCoy began indignantly. It was with a real effort that Kirk maintained the gravity that seemed appropriate to the old, familiar, comfortable occasion. And sure enough, Spock nodded politely to the outraged McCoy and returned to his station.

In the end, Kirk couldn't maintain it. He laughed—a laugh of delighted affection. To the smiling Sulu beside him, he said, "We're through here, Mr. Sulu. Warp factor three."

THE ENEMY WITHIN

(Richard Matheson)

The planet's desert terrain had yielded an interesting roundup of mineral and animal specimens, and Kirk was busy checking the containers for beam-up to the *Enterprise* when a gust of icy wind blew a spray of sand in his face. Beside him, Sulu, holding a meek doglike creature on a leash, shivered.

"Temperature's beginning to drop, Captain."

"Gets down to 250 degrees below at nightfall," Kirk said. He blinked the sand out of his eyes, stooped to pat Sulu's animal—and wheeled at the sound of a shout. Geological technician Fisher had fallen from the bank where he'd been working. From shoulders to feet his jumpsuit was smeared with a sticky, yellowish ore.

"Hurt yourself?" Kirk asked.

Fisher winced. "Cut my hand, sir."

It was a jagged, ugly cut. "Report to Sickbay," Kirk said.

Obediently Fisher removed his communicator from his belt. In the *Enterprise* Transporter Room, Scott, receiving his request for beam-up, said, "Right. Locked onto you." He turned to Transporter technician Wilson at the console. "Energize!" he ordered.

But as Fisher sparkled into shape on the platform, the console flashed a warning red light. "Coadjustor engagement," Scott said hastily. Wilson threw a switch. The red light faded.

Materialized, Fisher stepped off the platform.

"What happened?" Wilson asked.

"Took a flop," Fisher told him.

Wilson eyed the yellowish splatterings on his jumpsuit. Some lumps of the stuff had fallen from it to the platform's floor.

"Took a flop onto what?" Wilson asked.

"I don't know—some kind of soft ore."

Scott had reached for a scanner device. He ran it over the jumpsuit. "That ore's magnetic," he said. "Decontaminate your uniform, Fisher."

"Yes, sir."

Frowning, Scott examined the console. "It acted like a burnout," he grumbled to Wilson. "I don't like it."

Kirk's voice broke in on his concentration. "Captain Kirk, ready for beam-up."

"Just a moment, Captain." Scott tested the console again. "Seems to be OK now," he told Wilson. "But we can do with a double check. Get me a synchronic meter." Returning to his speaker, he said, "All right, Captain. Locked onto you." Then he activated the Transporter.

There was an unfamiliar whine in its humming. Hurriedly dialing it out, Scott decided to warn Kirk he was delaying the beam-up. But the process had already begun. The engineer looked anxiously toward the platform. In its dazzle Kirk stood on it, dazed-looking, unusually pale. As he stepped from it, his legs almost buckled. Scott ran to him. "What's wrong, Captain? Let me give you a hand."

"Just a little dizzy, that's all," Kirk said. "I'm sure it's nothing serious." He glanced around him. "You're not leaving the Transporter Room untended to look after me, are you?"

"No, sir. Wilson's just gone for a tool."

The door closed behind them. More sparkle appeared on the platform. A figure took shape on it. When it had gathered solidity, it could be seen as a perfect double of Kirk. Except for its eyes. They were those of a rabid animal just released from a cage.

It looked around it, tense, as though expecting attack.

Wilson opened the door. Immediately sensing that tension, "Captain," he said, "are you all right?"

His reply was a hoarse growl. The double glanced around it again seeking some means of escape. It licked its dry lips. Then it saw the door Wilson had left open.

Out in the corridor Kirk was saying, "I can manage now. You'd better get back to the Transporter Room, Scotty."

"Yes, sir."

"Thanks for the help."

"I wish you'd let Dr. McCoy give you a look-over, Captain."

"All right, Engineer. I'll have him check my engines."

He didn't have far to go. At the next cross passage he collided with McCoy. "I think we need a control signal at this cor—" McCoy broke off to stare at Kirk. "What's happened to you?"

"I don't know," Kirk said.

"You look like you ran into a wall."

"Is that your official diagnosis?"

"Never mind my diagnosis! Go and lie down. I have a malingerer to be treated. Then I'll come and check you."

"If you can find me," Kirk said—and moved on down the corridor. McCoy followed his going with puzzled eyes. Then he hastened on back to the waiting Fisher in Sickbay.

The soiled jumpsuit had been discarded. McCoy cleaned the cut hand. "Like to get off duty, wouldn't you?" he said. "Take a little vacation."

Fisher grinned. And McCoy, swabbing the wound, lifted his head at the sound of the opening door.

The double spoke at once. "*Brandy*," it said.

The demand, the manner, the whole bearing of replica Kirk was uncharacteristic of the real one. Fisher's presence put a brake on McCoy's amazement. He decided to ignore the demand. "Don't go running back to work now," he told Fisher. "Keep the bandage moist with this antiseptic. Take the bottle along with you."

"Yes, sir." Fisher held up his swathed hand, smiling at the double. "It isn't too bad, Captain."

The remark was ignored. McCoy turned to the double standing in the doorway and gestured to it to enter the office. "Sit down, Jim," he said. "I think we'd better . . ."

He stopped. The double had gone to the locked liquor cabinet, its nails clawing at it. *"I said brandy,"* it said.

McCoy stared, dumbfounded. The double was snarling now at its failure to pry open the cabinet's door. Nervous, uneasy, McCoy tried again. "Sit down, Jim."

A shudder passed through the double. A savage whisper broke from it. *"Give me the brandy!"*

"What is the *matter* with—" McCoy began. The clawing hands were lifting with the clear intention of smashing the cabinet's glass.

"Jim!" McCoy shouted.

The double whirled, crouched for a leap, its fists clenching. Instinctively McCoy recoiled from the coming blow. Then he recovered himself. "All right, I'll give you the brandy. Sit down!" But he didn't give the brandy. As he unlocked the cabinet door, he was shouldered aside—and the double, seizing a bottle of liquor, made for the door.

"Drink it in *your quarters*, Jim! I'll see you there in a . . ."

The door slammed shut.

McCoy, striding over to his viewing screen, flicked it on. Spock's face appeared. "Anything peculiar happen down on that planet's surface, Mr. Spock?"

The cool voice said, "One slight accident, Doctor, which I'm sure won't tax your miraculous healing powers."

But McCoy was too disturbed to rise to the bait. "Did it involve the Captain?"

"No."

"Well, there's something very wrong with him. He just left my office after carrying on like a wild man."

The wild man, rampaging down the corridor, suddenly had a mind to private drinking. A sign over a door declared it to be the entrance to the quarters of Yeoman Janice Rand. The double touched it, conceiving unmentionable notions—and slipped through the door. Inside, it uncorked the bottle. Tipping it up, it gulped down the brandy in deep swallows. Then it grunted in pure, voluptuous pleasure. The bite of the brandy down its throat was too seductive to resist the

impulse to swallow some more. Eyes half-shut in sensu-
al delight, its face was the face of a Kirk released from
all repressions, all self-discipline and moral order.

Kirk himself had not entirely recovered from his
mysterious vertigo. Alone in his quarters, he had his
shirt off, and was flexing his neck and shoulder muscles
to rid his head of the whirling inside it. When the
knock came at his door, he said, "Yes?"

"Spock, sir."

"Come in," Kirk said, pressing the door's unlocking
button.

"Dr. McCoy asked me to check on you, sir."

Shouldering back into his shirt, Kirk said, "Why
you?"

"Only Dr. McCoy could answer that, Captain."

"He must have had a reason."

"One would assume so," Spock said mildly, his keen
eyes on Kirk's face.

"Well, Mr. Spock? I hope you know me next time
we meet."

"Dr. McCoy said you were acting like a wild man."

"McCoy said that?" Kirk paused. "He must have
been joking."

"I'll get back to the bridge now," Spock said.

"I'll tell McCoy you were here."

As the door closed, Kirk, puzzled by the interchange, reached for his Captain's coat.

On Deck 12, corridors above him, his double was
feeling the effects of the brandy. But at the sound of a
door sliding open, it was sober enough to take hiding in
the bedroom of Yeoman Rand's quarters. It watched
her enter. When she had placed her tricorder on a
table, it stepped forward into her full sight.

It was not Kirk's custom to visit the bedrooms of
attractive female members of his crew. Janice was shak-
en by his appearance in hers. She decided to smile.
"This is an unexpected pleasure, sir," she said gamely.

The smile faltered at the suggestive leer she received.
"Is there something I can—?" Then she tensed. The

double had come so close to her she could smell the brandy on its breath. She flushed at such male nearness, fought back an uprush of embarrassed apprehension and said, "Is there—can I do something for you, Captain?"

"You bet you can," the double grinned. "But Jim will do here, Janice."

Neither the words nor the tone fitted the image of Kirk that existed in the mind of Janice Rand. She had never seen him anything but coolly courteous toward women members of his crew. Since the day she had joined it, she had thought of him as the unobtainable but most desirable man she'd ever met. However, that was her own secret. It just wasn't possible that he *was* obtainable, not Captain James T. Kirk of the Starship *Enterprise*. And by a twenty-year-old, obscure yeoman named Janice Rand. He'd been drinking, of course; and when men drank . . . Nevertheless, of all the women on the ship, this handsomest man in the world had sought her out; and by some miraculous quirk of circumstance seemed to be finding her worthy of his sexual interest. She suddenly felt that she, along with her uniform, had gone transparent.

"I—Captain, this isn't—" she stammered.

"You're too much woman not to know," the double said. "I've been mad for you since the day you joined the ship. We both know what's been inside us all this time. We can't say no to it—not any more, not when we're finally alone, just you and me. Just try to deny it—after this . . . "

It swept her into its arms, kissing her hard on the lips. For a moment she was immobilized by the shock. Then she pulled back. "*Please*, Captain. You—we . . ."

The handsome face tightened with anger. She was kissed again harshly; and with a little moan, she tried to pull free. She was jerked closer. Now the kisses pressed against her throat, her neck.

"You're—hurting me," she whispered.

"Then don't fight me. You know you don't want to."

She stared into what she thought were Kirk's eyes. In some shameful way it was true. She *didn't* want to fight the Captain's kisses. Only how dare he presume to know it?

"Shall I make that an order, Yeoman Rand?"

This time the kiss on her mouth was openly brutal. Janice, infuriated by exposure of a truth she wanted neither to know herself nor be known to anyone else, began to fight in earnest. She scratched the double across its handsome face. It pulled back; and she dashed for the door. She was grabbed as it opened—but out in the corridor, Fisher, returning to his room with the antiseptic liquid he'd forgotten, had seen the struggling pair.

"On your way!" It was Kirk's command voice.

Relief surged through Janice. *The Captain had implicated himself in this disgraceful scene.* If there was penalty to pay in loss of his crew's respect, he'd have only himself to blame. She screamed, "Call Mr. Spock!"

Fisher gaped at her. *"Call Mr. Spock!"* she screamed again. Fisher broke into a run. The double tightened its hold on her. Then, realizing how the witness menaced it, it rushed out into the corridor.

Fisher made it to a wall intercom. "This is Fisher of Geology! Come to Deck 12, Section . . . "

The double caught him in midsentence. Fisher was spun around to take a smashing right to his jaw. It was his turn to scream. "Help! Section 3!"

The scream came through to the bridge. Spock bolted for the elevator, shouting "Take over!" to navigator Farrell.

Deck 12 was deserted. Spock hesitated. Then, starting down the corridor, he slowed his run to a wary walk, his sharp Vulcan eyes searching. After a moment, he stooped to run a finger along a dark streak on the flooring. When he looked at the finger, it was red, wet with blood.

Its trail of drops led to the quarters of Yeoman Rand. He opened the door. She was sitting on a chair, her uniform disheveled, her eyes blank, stunned. Near her, Fisher lay on the floor. She didn't speak as Spock bent down to him. His face was a mass of mangled flesh and blood.

"Who did this to you?" Spock asked.

Fisher's torn lips moved. "Captain Kirk," he whispered. Then he subsided into unconsciousness.

Kirk asked his question very quietly. "And Yeoman Rand says I assaulted her?"

"Yes, sir," Spock said. "And technician Fisher also accuses you of assault upon her and himself."

"I've been here in my quarters for the past half hour," Kirk said.

Spock held up the nearly empty brandy bottle.

"What's that?" Kirk said.

"The bottle of brandy Dr. McCoy says you took from his office cabinet. I found it in Yeoman Rand's room with Fisher."

"McCoy says *I* took that brandy?" The whirling in Kirk's head had come back. He shut his eyes against its wheeling stars. Then he rose. "Let's find out what's going on in this ship." He moved past Spock into the corridor.

The elevator door closed behind them—and the double, a darker shadow in the shadows of a cross passage, slipped quietly out into the corridor. Panting, it pried at the door of Kirk's quarters. It got it open. Inside, the lock on the panel of the sleeping compartment caught its eye. It depressed the unlocking button. It relocked the panel behind it and fell across the bed, sighing with exhaustion. Then it buried the replica of Kirk's face in a pillow to shut out the sights and sounds of a world that hated it.

In Sickbay, Yeoman Rand was saying, "Then he kissed me—and said we—that he was the Captain and could order me to—" Her eyes were on her cold hands, safer to look at than Kirk's face. She had addressed her words to Spock.

"Go on," Kirk said.

She looked at him now. "I—I didn't know what to do. When you started talking about—us—about the feeling we've been—hiding all this time . . . "

"The feeling you and I have been hiding, Yeoman Rand?" Kirk said. "Do I understand you correctly?"

"Yes, sir." In desperation she twisted around to McCoy. "He *is* the Captain, Doctor! I couldn't just—" Her face tightened. "I couldn't *talk* to you!" she burst out at Kirk. "I had to fight you, scratch your face and kick and . . ."

"Yeoman Rand," Kirk said. He went over to her, pretending not to notice how she shrank from his approach. "Look at me! Look at my face! Do you see any scratches on it?"

"No, sir," she whispered.

"I have been in my quarters, Yeoman. How could I have been with you and in my own quarters at one and the same time?"

She wrung her hands. "But—" Her voice broke. "I know what happened. And it *was* you. I—I don't want to get you into trouble. I wouldn't even have mentioned it if technician Fisher hadn't seen you, too, and . . . "

"Yeoman," Kirk said, "it wasn't *me!*"

She began to cry. She looked very small, very young in her rumpled uniform. Kirk reached out a compassionate hand to her shoulder—but she shied away from his touch as though it might burn her.

Spock said, "You can go now, Yeoman."

Sobbing, she got to her feet. As she reached the door, Kirk said, "Yeoman." She stopped. "*It was not me,*" he repeated. But she went on out the door without looking back.

Spock broke the silence. "Captain, there is an impostor aboard this ship."

It was to be expected from Spock. Faith to the end—that was Spock. Kirk pulled his uniform collar away from his neck as though it were choking him. After a moment he went to the door of Sickbay's treatment room where McCoy had gone back to work on the battered Fisher. He was busy, of course; too busy with Fisher to look at him. But the prone Fisher looked at him from the sheeted table—and in his eyes there was open scorn.

The intercom buzzed; and Scott said, "Captain, can we see you in the Transporter Room for a minute?"

Kirk took the scalding memory of Fisher's look with him. If Spock hadn't silently joined him, he wondered if he'd have found the courage to respond to Scott's call. Had he, too, heard the interesting details of his Captain's recent activities? But Scott's total concern seemed to be the still defective Transporter. He looked up from the console as Kirk entered. "It's a complete breakdown, Captain." He turned his head to say to his technicians, "Continue circuit testing." The meek, doglike creature collected from the planet was lying beside the console. Scott pointed to it. "We beamed this animal up to the ship, sir, and . . ."

"And what?" Kirk said.

Scott paused. "The animal is here. But it's also over there in that specimen case."

He left the console to go over to the case with Kirk and Spock. A fierce growl greeted them. Scott cautiously lifted the lid. The beast inside bared its teeth, its lips flecked with the foam of its fury. Scott hastily dropped the lid over its leap at them.

"It appears to be the twin of the other animal," Spock said slowly. "Except for the difference in temperament, they might be one and the same."

Scott had hurried back to the console to pick up the quiet creature. Stroking it, he said, "A few seconds after they sent this one up through the Transporter, that duplicate of it appeared on the platform. If this had happened to a man—it's some kind of opposite."

The intentness on Kirk's face was naked. Scott went on. "One beast gentle like this—and one savage, wolfish, this one and *that* one—some kind of ferocious *opposite*. Captain, till we know what's gone wrong with the Transporter, we dare not use it to beam up the landing party!"

"Oh, my God . . . "

The whisper was wrenched from Kirk by the force of sudden revelation. It was no impostor who was loose on the *Enterprise*. What was loose on it was his own counterpart—the dark, brutish aspect of human nature which every mortal carries within him from birth to the grave. His Cain was roaming the *Enterprise* in a mindless, murderous search for a vengeance that would appease the bitterness of years of denial—the years it had spent as a prisoner of conscience, of duty, of

responsibility. Somehow it had got free from its embod-
iment in him, and wearing his face, using his voice,
wandering his ship, had found its release.

He gradually became conscious of Spock's eyes. The
Vulcan had taken the lamb-gentle animal into his arms.
Something in the way he held it stilled the turmoil in
Kirk's soul. He was able to speak.

"Do you know what caused the animal to divide in
two, Scotty?"

"We think we do, sir. When Fisher came up, his
clothes were splashed with some soft, yellowish stuff.
He said it was ore. Some of it fell on the Transporter
platform. When we scanned it, we found it contained
unknown magnetic elements. Maybe it caused an over-
load. We can't tell—not yet."

"Is the Transporter working at all?"

"Yes, sir. But to use it to bring up the landing
party—they might all be duplicated like you—" He
caught himself. "Like the animal, Captain."

So Scott *had* heard. "How long will it take to locate
the trouble?"

"Can't say, sir."

Kirk fought for calm, for reason. "We can't just leave
those four men down there. They'll freeze to death. At
night that planet's temperature sinks to 250 degrees
below zero."

"We're doing everything we can, Captain!"

Kirk looked at the Transporter platform. What was
the secret it refused to divulge? He'd emerged from it
whole, unsplit, a thousand times. Why not this last
time? *What had happened?* When and how had he been
divided in two halves like a one-celled organism repro-
ducing itself? The whirling in his head was back once
more. And the platform looked back at him, empty, its
secret still withheld.

Spock had come to stand beside him. "About this
double of yours, Captain."

Kirk started like a man aroused from nightmare.
"Yes, we've got to find him. Search parties, Mr. Spock
—we've got to organize search parties."

"We can't risk killing it," Spock said. "We have no

data—no way of knowing the effect of its death on you."

So Spock understood. "Yes, that's right," Kirk said. "We don't know that—but the men must be armed. All men to be armed with phasers locked to the stun setting. He's to be taken without—if anyone fires to kill, he won't die—it's not the way to get rid of him . . . "

Spock noted the breaks between thoughts and words. They were disjointed, disorganized. No, there was no doubt. This Kirk was not the integrated, decisive Kirk he knew.

"It will be difficult to order the search parties to capture a being who so closely resembles you, Captain."

"Tell them—" Kirk looked at him helplessly. "I'd better make an announcement to the entire crew—tell them what's happened as well as I can. It's a good crew—they deserve to be told."

"I must object, sir," Spock said. "You are the Captain of this ship. You cannot afford to appear vulnerable in the eyes of your crew. It is your damnable fate to have to seem perfect to them. I'm sorry, sir. Yet that is the fact. They lose their confidence in you—and you lose your command."

Kirk pressed his forehead between his hands. "I know that, Mr. Spock. Why did I forget it?" He turned away, then stopped without looking back. "If you see me slipping again, your order is to *tell* me so."

"Yes, Captain."

His back stiff, Kirk walked out of the Transporter Room. In the bridge he touched the back of his command chair before he took his position in it. Command —no weakness, no fault, no hesitation. Bracing himself for the front of perfection, he flicked on his intercom. "This is the Captain speaking. There is an impostor aboard this ship—a man who looks exactly like me and is pretending to *be* me. The man is dangerous. Utmost caution is to be observed. All crew members are to arm themselves. The impostor may be identified by scratches on his face."

The message reached the double. It sat up quickly on Kirk's bed. "Repeat," came the voice from the intercom. "The impostor may be identified by scratches on his face. Search parties will report to Mr. Spock for assignment. All hand phasers will be set to stun force. The impostor is not to be injured. Repeat. The impostor is not to be injured."

The double touched the scratches on its face. Then it got up to go to the mirror and stare at its reflection. "Impostor!" it muttered to itself. "*I'm Kirk!*" it shouted at Kirk's image on the intercom viewing screen. A gust of fury shook it. It seized a metal box from the dresser and hurled it at the screen. The sound of crashing glass frightened it. "I'm Kirk," it whimpered to its reflection in the mirror. The scratches showed red, unhealed. To examine them more closely, it pushed aside a jar of medicated cream. The loosened lid fell off. The double dug its fingers into the cream, looked once more at the scratches and began to rub the cream into them. It made them feel better. It also hid the weals. The double grunted with satisfaction. It was dabbing more of the concealing cream into the cuts when it heard running sounds from the corridor outside.

When the sounds had gone, it unlocked the door. Moving out into the working area of Kirk's quarters, it slid its entrance panel half open. Wilson, carrying some Transporter equipment, was hurrying down the corridor.

"Wilson!" the double called. "Come here!"

Wilson came.

"Give me your weapon belt!"

"Yes, sir."

As he handed over the belt, Wilson saw the smeared cream on its face. But his suspicion came too late. The double had the phaser out of the belt. It struck him on the jaw with its butt. When Wilson fell, it stooped to pound his jaw with the heavy butt. Then it dragged him into Kirk's cabin. The bloody phaser still in hand, it nodded to itself—and walked casually out into the corridor.

Down on the planet's surface it was growing dark. Sulu and his three crewmen were gathering rocks to erect a wall against the rising wind. Frost had already whitened the dismal landscape as far as they could see.

Over his communicator, Kirk said, "Mr. Sulu, how is the rock shelter coming?"

"It's a compliment to these rocks, sir, to call them a shelter. It's down to 50 below zero now, Captain."

They were not equipped with thermal clothing. It was hard to say, "Kirk out." He might better have said, "Kirk down and out." That was the truth. In his command chair, he had to steady himself against another attack of vertigo. "We've got to get those men up!" he said to Spock. But Spock was taking a report from one of his search parties. "Deck 5 Sections 2 and 3 completely covered now, sir. Result, negative. Proceeding to Sections 4 and 5."

"Acknowledged," Spock said and flicked off his audio—but only to flick it on again to another intercom call.

"Search party number eight, sir. Transporter technician Wilson has just been found crawling out of the Captain's cabin. He's been badly beaten. He says the impostor attacked him, called him by his name and took his phaser."

"Get him to Sickbay," Spock said. "Then continue your search."

"We must locate this—this opposite of mine before he—" Kirk broke off. "But how, Spock, how?"

"It is apparent, sir, that it possesses your knowledge of the ship, its crew and devices. That being so, perhaps we can foresee its next move. Knowing how this ship is constructed, where would *you* go to elude a mass search, Captain?"

For the first time since his disaster, Kirk spoke without hesitation. "The lower level. The Engineering deck. Let's go!"

In the elevator Spock removed his phaser from his belt. Without looking at Kirk, he said, "I'm setting this, not to the kill cycle, but to the stun one, sir. What about your phaser?" Kirk took the hint; and Spock said, "This thing is dangerous. Don't you think we'll need some help if we find it?"

The torture of indecision was back. Finally Kirk said, "No. If we find him, I don't want anyone else around but you." He had stepped out of the elevator when Spock called, *"Captain!"*

Kirk turned.

Spock said, "You ordered me to tell you . . . "

"I said *no*, Mr. Spock. No one but you."

The lower level of the Engineering deck held the vast complex that powered the *Enterprise*. It was a cavern of shadows, broken by glints of gleaming machinery, its passageways narrowing, widening, narrowing again to crisscross other passages. The droning hum of its huge nuclear energizers reverberated against its metal walls. Suddenly, as he rounded a dynamo, Spock realized he was alone. He turned to retrace his steps in hope of locating Kirk again.

Kirk, unaware he had lost Spock, looked at the phaser he held at the ready. The sight of it repelled him. A suicide weapon was what it was. The life it would fell was part of his own. He replaced the phaser in his belt.

And his Cain saw him do it. Crouched between two power generators, the double had heard his approaching footsteps. Its features tensed with its curious mixture of fear and ferocity. Its phaser aimed, it moved away from its shelter for a full confrontation.

Kirk stopped dead. As he recognized his own face in the Other's face, a chill passed over him. This nameless Thing belonged to him more utterly than any name his parents had given him. The two Kirks stared at each other in a kind of trance. Then, as though he were drawn by a power as unknown as it was powerful, Kirk stepped toward his double. It raised its phaser.

Kirk spoke. His voice sounded strange in his own ears. It was solemn with the prophetic tone of a mystic suddenly endowed with an incontrovertible truth. "You must not hurt me," he said. "You must not kill me. You can live only as long as I live."

Uncertainty flickered over the double's face; and Kirk, in a kind of dream, knew he was seeing the reflection of his own new uncertainty.

Then the hesitation faded. *"I* don't need you!" the double said. "I don't have to believe what you say. So I *can* kill you!"

Its finger was on the kill trigger. Leaping, the momentum of his leap lending force to his clenched fist, Spock lunged from behind the generator to land it, hammerlike, on the double's chin. It fell. Its phaser fired, the beam striking a machine unit behind Kirk. It flared into glow and collapsed.

Spock looked down at the sprawled double. "I fear," he said, "that the ministrations of Dr. McCoy will be needed."

The fear was well-founded. Consciousness was reluctant to return to the double. Each in his different way anxious, Kirk and Spock watched McCoy as he stooped over the still figure in its bed. McCoy worked silently. After a moment, Kirk went to the viewing screen. Turning it on to Engineering, he said, "What about those Transporter circuits, Scotty? They're all checked through now, aren't they?"

"Yes, sir. And we thought we'd corrected the trouble. But now something else has gone wrong."

"*What?*" Kirk demanded.

"We don't know, sir. We're working on it. Is that all, Captain?"

Once more Kirk was unable to rally either a yes or a no. There was an uncomfortable pause. Finally Scott said, "Then I'd better get back to work, sir."

It would be darker on the planet. Kirk cried out, "Find out what's wrong, Scott! And fix it in God's name! Four human lives are depending on that Transporter!"

Scott said stiffly, "We're doing our best, sir."

Kirk leaned his forehead against the frame of the viewing screen. "I know, Scotty. You always do your best. Keep me posted, will you?"

"Yes, sir." The voice had relaxed.

Over at the bed, McCoy had completed his examination. "How is—he?" Kirk asked.

"Pulse and blood pressure high," McCoy said. He glanced at Spock. "Probably due to that sock on the chin."

"It was necessary, Doctor."

"This—creature will be recovering consciousness

soon. As I have no idea at all about its mental state, I can't give it a tranquilizer. I think we'd better bind it."

He looked at Kirk for authorization. Kirk was suddenly oppressed by a sense of suffocation. The heavy tonnage of command responsibility seemed to be crushing him. He shook his head to try and clear it of the dizziness. "Yes," he said, "all right. I just wish someone would tell me what's the matter with *me*."

"You are losing the power of decision, Captain," Spock said.

"What?"

McCoy was busy binding the double but not so busily that he couldn't direct a glare at Spock. But the Vulcan continued, cool and unruffled. "Judging from my observations," he said, "you are rapidly losing your capacity for action. There's hesitation in time of crises—loss of perception. Captain, you refuse to defend yourself. You refused to demand adequate assistance when we went down to the Engineering level whereas you should have placed yourself in guarded isolation until the impostor was captured." He paused. "You have dismissed men for less hesitation, less passivity in the face of danger."

"Make your point, Spock!" shouted McCoy.

"Point?"

"You *have* one, I presume," McCoy said.

"I am analyzing, Doctor; not point-making."

"It's the Captain's guts you're analyzing! Are you aware of that, Mr. Spock?"

"Vituperation, Doctor?"

Composed, unmoved, Spock went on. "The dichotomies inherent in the human mind are multiple," he said. "The problem of command, for instance, highly pertinent in this case. Command is a balance between positive and negative energies—an equilibrium of the forces generated by each of these energies. The proof?"

He turned to Kirk. "Your negative energy was removed from you by that duplication process. Thus, the power of command has begun to fail you. Things remaining as they are, how long can you continue to function as Captain of this ship? Finally unable to decide anything at all, will you . . . "

McCoy broke in. "Jim, give him a command! Tell him to get lost!"

"If I seem emotionally insensitive to the agony of your ordeal, Captain, please understand. It's the way I am."

"That's for damned sure!" yelled McCoy.

"*Gentlemen*," Kirk said. In the end, always in the end, one's pain remained a private matter. The scene, however dismal, was always enacted alone. He smiled wryly at them. "I may be losing my ability to command but it hasn't entirely disappeared. Until it does, you will both kindly knock it off."

The intercom on McCoy's desk whirred. Kirk flicked it on. "Kirk here."

"Engineering, sir. We've just located that new trouble with the Transporter. Its Ionizer Unit has been mangled. Looks as if a phaser beam had hit it."

The double's phaser beam had hit it, the double, that separated part of himself. If his crewmen died their lonely death on the subarctic planet beneath him, it would be he, Kirk, their trusted Captain who had killed them.

He got up to walk to the door. "If I'm needed," he said, "I'll be in the Briefing Room."

They had lit a fire down on the planet. Black night was spreading toward them from its horizon. And the stealthy fronds of frost were creeping over the rocks of the rock shelter where the abandoned crewmen huddled together for warmth. Sulu, his lips cracked and sore, had to hold his hands over the fire before his fingers could manipulate his communicator. "Can you give us a status report, *Enterprise*? It's fallen to 90 degrees below zero down here."

"This is the Captain, Mr. Sulu. We have located the trouble. It shouldn't be much longer."

"Think you could rig up a cord, sir, and lower us down a pot of coffee?"

"I'll see what I can do about that," Kirk said.

"Rice wine will do, sir, if you're short of coffee."

"I'll check the commissariat for rice wine, Mr. Sulu." And once more it had to be "Kirk out."

He watched his hand reach out to the intercom button. He was afraid to call Scott. He pressed the button. "That mangled unit, Scotty. Status report."

"Nothing much of it left, sir."

"How bad is it?"

"We can't repair it in less than a week."

A week. One hundred and sixty-eight hours. Death by cold was said to be preceded by sleep. Alone in the Briefing Room, Kirk realized that imagination had become his mortal enemy. It showed him the planet's surface under the deadly grip of its incredible cold, its night ominous with the coming sleep of death as the blood in his men's veins turned to ice. They'd be moving slowly now if they could move at all . . .

Reality endorsed imagination. Sulu was slowed to a crawl as he elbowed himself to the dying warmth to check his phaser. He fired it at another boulder. It burst into glow. The others inched toward it; and Sulu made his frost-blackened lips say, "That rice wine is taking too long. I'm giving Room Service another call."

Nobody spoke as he opened his communicator. "*Enterprise*, this is Sulu."

"Kirk here, Mr. Sulu."

"Hot line direct to the Captain again. Are we that far gone, sir?"

Kirk struck the Briefing Room table with his fist. "Everybody but you's got the afternoon off. I'm watching the store. How is it down there?"

"Lovely," Sulu said. "We're using our phasers to heat the rocks. One phaser's quit on us. Three are still operational. Any chance of getting us aboard before the skiing season opens down here?"

The ice—maybe it would be merciful, quick. *Think.* But he couldn't think. His thoughts like comets that would not be stayed flashed through his mind—and were gone . . .

He felt no surprise to see Spock quietly lift the speaker he had dropped.

"This is Spock, Mr. Sulu. You will hold out a little longer. *Hold out.* Survival procedures, Mr. Sulu."

"As per your training program, Mr. Spock."

"Yes, Mr. Sulu."

Kirk reached for the speaker. "Sulu—just don't drift, don't lose—awareness. Sulu, beware of sleep . . . "

As Spock said, "Spock out," Kirk felt an irresistible impulse to return to Sickbay. He wasn't entirely composed of that atavism that had destroyed the Ionizer Unit. He was Captain James T. Kirk of the Starship *Enterprise*, too—and he was going back to Sickbay. Courage was doing what you were afraid to do.

The consciousness that had come back to the double was a thing of howling panic. It was thrusting madly against the net of cords that held it, the force of its screams swelling the veins of its neck. As he watched the writhing body on the bed, it seemed to Kirk that he could taste the acid of its frenzy in his mouth. How he knew what he knew he didn't know; but he knew that the double was feeling some ultimate terror it had met in the black labyrinth of its Cain fate.

"It should be calming down," McCoy said, laying a hypodermic aside. "This tranquilizer should be working now." He threw a worried glance at the body function panel. All its readings showed a dangerous peak.

The tormented body on the bed strained again at its bonds. A shudder shook it. Then, suddenly, it collapsed, its head lolling like a broken doll's.

"What's happened?" Kirk cried. The readings on the body-function panel were rapidly falling.

"The tranquilizer was a mistake," McCoy said. "Its system has rejected it."

"He's not—*dying?*" Kirk said.

McCoy spoke tonelessly. "Yes, it is."

"No," Kirk whispered. "No." He reached for McCoy's arm. "I can't survive without him and he can't survive without me."

McCoy shook his head; and the double moaned. "Afraid, afraid," it said.

Kirk went to it. "Help me," it wept. "I am afraid—so afraid."

Kirk took its hand. McCoy started forward. "Jim, you'd better not . . . "

Kirk stooped over the bed. "Don't be afraid. This is my hand. Feel it. Hold on to it. That's it. Hang on to my hand. I won't let you go."

"Afraid," whimpered the double pitifully.

Some strength rose up from unknown depths in Kirk. It was as though he had lived through just such a scene before. The words that came to him seemed familiar. "You must hold on to me because we've been pulled apart. Come back! No, you're letting go! Hold on to me. Tight! Tighter!"

He lifted the sheet to wipe the sweat from its forehead. "I'm pulling you back to me. We need each other! That's it. *Tight*! We have to hang on—together . . ."

McCoy, at the body-function panel, looked around, astounded. But all Kirk saw were the tragic eyes fixed on his in abject dependence. "No fear," he said. "You can come back. You are not afraid. *You are not afraid*. Be back with me. Be back, be back, be back . . ."

McCoy touched his shoulder. "Jim, it *is* back."

Kirk stumbled over to McCoy's desk, slumping into its chair. "Now *you* can use some brandy," McCoy said.

He gagged on the drink. Eyes shut, he said, "I must take him back—into myself. I don't want to, Bones—a brutish, mindless wolf in human shape. But I must. He is me, *me!*"

"Jim, don't take this so hard," McCoy said. "We are all part wolf and part lamb. We need both parts. Compassion is reconciliation between them. It is human to be both lamb and wolf."

"Human?" Kirk asked bitterly.

"Yes, *human*. Some of his wolfishness makes you the man you are. God forbid that I should ever agree with Spock—but he was right! Without the strength of the wolf in you, you could not command this ship! And without the lamb in you, your discipline would be harsh and cruel. Jim, you just used the lamb to give life back to that dying wolf . . ."

The double was listening, concentrated.

The intercom buzzed. Drained, Kirk said, "Kirk here."

"Spock, sir. Will you come to the Transporter Room? We think we may have found an answer."

"I'm on my way," Kirk said. He turned to McCoy. "Thanks, Bones. And keep your fingers crossed."

"Tell Mr. Spock I'm shaking all my rattles to invoke good spirits."

But as the door closed behind Kirk, there came a cry from the bed. *"No!"* The startled McCoy went to the bed. The double was sitting up. It said quietly, "No. *Everything is under control right now."*

In the Transporter Room, Wilson was holding the mild doglike creature.

"What's that answer you think you've found?" Kirk asked.

"A way to make the Transporter safe, sir," Scott said. "We have attached some temporary bypass and leader circuits to compensate for the velocity variation. There shouldn't be more than a five-point difference in speed balance."

"Our suggestion is that we send the two animals through the Transporter," Spock said.

So that was the answer—hope that amendment in the Transporter would somehow rejoin the two halves of the animal as it had somehow cut them apart. It was hoped that his dying men could be beamed home to the *Enterprise* without risk of the fatal division. Hope. Well, without it, you couldn't live.

"All right," Kirk said. "Go ahead."

Spock took the hypodermic from the top of the Transporter console. He nodded at Scott. The Chief Engineer went to the specimen case and lifted its lid. "I'll grab it by the scruff of its neck and hold it as still as I can." He reached into the case. The snarling beast twisted and writhed against Scott's grip on its neck.

"Don't hurt it!" Kirk cried.

Injecting the shot, Spock said, "It's painless, Captain, quick. The animal will lose consciousness for only the few, necessary moments." The snarls subsided. Spock took the creature from Scott and carried it to the Transporter platform where Wilson was waiting with the other one. They laid them on the platform, side by side. Scott, at the console, said, "If this doesn't work—" He broke off at Spock's signal. He turned a dial. The platform flared into glow. The two animals vanished and the glow faded.

"Energize to reverse," Spock said.

Scott twisted a dial. The platform flared into light again. The two animals reappeared—and the light dimmed.

Spock ran to the console. He made some adjustment of dials. "Again," he said to Scott. The process was repeated. The energizing dial was reversed. The platform broke into dazzle. As it shaped itself into substance, McCoy came in.

One animal lay on the platform.

"It's dead," Kirk said.

"Not so fast, Jim," McCoy said.

Kirk waited while he checked the limp body for heartbeat. There was none. Into the silence Spock said, "The shock—the shock of reabsorption . . . "

Kirk stumbled out of the Transporter Room.

Later, in Sickbay, McCoy gave tentative support to Spock's diagnosis of the cause of the death. Straightening up from the table that held the dead beast, he said, "Maybe it *was* the shock of reabsorption that killed it. But it would take a post mortem before we could even approach certainty."

"Why shock?" Kirk asked.

"We're only guessing, Jim."

"Yes, I know. But you've both used the word shock."

"The consequence of instinctive fear," Spock said. "The animal lacked the ability to understand the process of reabsorption. Its fear was so great it induced shock. Other conditions that cause shock are not apparent." He was carefully examining the creature. "You yourself can see, sir, that the body is quite undamaged."

Kirk was groping for some answer of his own. "*He*—in that bed in there—felt great fear." He turned to McCoy. "You saw him feel it. But he survived it. He *survived* it!"

"Just by a hairsbreadth," McCoy reminded him. "I can hear it coming, Jim. You want to take this double of yours through the Transporter with you—you and it, *with* it. No, Jim, *no!*"

"Four of my men are freezing to death," Kirk said.

"But there isn't one genuine shred of evidence to prove this animal died of fear! Shock? Yes. But fear? That's mere theory!"

"Based on the laws of probability," Spock said.

"Probability be hanged!" McCoy shouted. "It's Jim's life that's at stake! And all of a sudden you're an expert on fear! That's a base emotion, Mr. Spock. What do you know about it?"

"I must remind you, Doctor, that I am half human," Spock said. "I am more aware than you of what it means to live with a divided spirit—of the suffering involved in possession of two separate selves. I survive it daily."

"That may be—but a piece of machinery is the problem. What do the laws of probability say about the Transporter? Is it reliable? You don't know! It's just more theory, more hopeful guesswork!"

Kirk said, "I am going through the Transporter with him."

McCoy threw up his arms in a gesture of hopelessness. "You've got more guts than brains, Jim! Use your head, for God's sake!"

"I'm getting my four men back on this ship," Kirk said. "And we can't risk using that Transporter until we know whether this animal died of fear—or mechanical malfunction in the Transporter."

"I want to save the men, too, Jim! But you're more vital to this ship than four crew members. That's the brutal truth—and you know it!"

Listening, Kirk felt his weakened will sink to its final depth of hesitation. "I have to—try. I must be allowed to try. If I don't try, their death is sure. So will mine be. I shall look alive, Bones. But I shall live as a half man. What good to this ship is a half man Captain?

"Jim, do me one favor. Before you decide, let me run an autopsy on this animal."

"Delay is too expensive," Kirk said.

"At least give Spock more time to test the Transporter. And let me get the lab started on the autopsy."

McCoy gathered up the dead animal in a sheet. "Wait, Jim, please wait." He hurried out of Sickbay.

Spock said, "I'll put the Transporter through another check-out cycle as soon as the Doctor returns."

Kirk whirled on him. "I don't need nursemaids, Mr. Spock!"

"As soon as the Doctor returns." The six words too many, Spock thought. The weakened will had finally steeled itself to decision only to meet doubt, argument, pressure. Those last six words had been a mistake.

"If you will excuse me, Captain," he said.

Kirk nodded. He watched Spock go. Half human, Spock—but you never came to the end of his aware humanity. Gratitude heartened him to do what he had to do. He was turning toward Sickbay's bed section when Sulu's voice sounded from the wall speaker.

"Kirk here, Mr. Sulu."

The voice was a whisper. "Captain—the rocks are cold—no phasers left—one of us is unconscious—we can't hold out much longer." The communicator crackled. "Captain—the cold is freezing the communicator—no time left—no time . . ."

The whisper fell silent. There was another crackle from the dead communicator. Kirk sank down on the double's bed. Four lives at risk on the fatal planet—two lives at risk in the Transporter process. There was no alternative.

The double spoke fearfully. "What are you going to do?"

Kirk didn't answer. He began to untie the cords of the restraining net over the bed. The double reached out and touched the phaser at his belt. "You don't need that," it said. "I'm not going to fight you any more. What are you going to do?"

"We are going through the Transporter together," Kirk said.

The double tensed. Then it controlled itself. "If that's what you want," it said.

"It's what I have to want," Kirk said. He untied the last cord, stepped back and raised his phaser. Staggering, the double got up. Then it leaned back against the bed for support. "I feel so weak," it said. "I'll be glad when this is over."

"Let's go," Kirk said.

The double moved toward the door; but on its first step it faltered, groaning. It tried again, staggered again—and Kirk instinctively reached out to help it. It saw its chance. Lunging, it drove its shoulder into Kirk, knocking him backward. The phaser dropped. It stooped for it. Recovering his balance, Kirk shouted, "No, no, you can't . . . "

The phaser butt crashed into the side of his head. He fell back on the bed. The double paused to finger the scratches on its face. McCoy's medication covered them. It smiled to itself. Then it began to strap Kirk into the bed. "I'm *you*," it told him.

Swaggering, it walked out into the corridor. At its end the elevator door slid open. Janice Rand was standing inside it. At once it tempered its swagger to a quiet walk.

"How are you, Yeoman Rand?"

"Captain," the girl said nervously.

It smiled at her. "Is that a question? No, I am not the impostor. Are you feeling better?"

"Yes, sir. Thank you."

"Good."

Maybe it was her opportunity, Janice thought. She'd done this man a grave injustice. "Captain," she said, "I've wanted to apologize. If I caused you . . ."

She got Kirk's own grin. "That's a big word—'if.' I understand, Yeoman. I hope you do. I owe you, I think, a personal explanation."

"No," she said. "It's I who owe you . . . "

"Let's call it a clarification, then," the double said. "I trust your discretion. There was no impostor, not really. The Transporter malfunctioned. It seems to have created a duplicate of me. It's hard to understand because we haven't yet determined what went wrong. But what we *do* know I'll explain to you later. You're entitled to that. All right?"

Bewildered, she nodded. "All right, sir."

The elevator door opened. Politely, the double stepped back, gesturing her forward. As the elevator moved on up to the bridge deck, it shouted with laughter. Slamming its hand against the elevator wall, it yelled, *"My* ship! Mine—all mine!"

The sight of Kirk's command chair intoxicated it. As it settled back into it, a frowning Farrell spoke from the navigation console. "No word from Mr. Sulu, Captain."

It ignored the comment; and Spock, hurrying over to the command chair, said, "Captain, I couldn't find you in the Transporter Room."

"I changed my mind," the double said. "Take your station, Mr. Spock." It didn't look at the Vulcan.

Spock walked slowly back to his computer. It was a very sudden change of mind for a mind that had struggled so valiantly for decision.

"Prepare to leave orbit, Mr. Farrell!"

If the order had commanded activation of the Destruct unit, its impact could not have been more devastating. Farrell stared in stark unbelief. The double became abruptly aware that every eye in the bridge was fixed on it.

"Captain—" Farrell began.

"I gave you an order, Mr. Farrell."

"I know, sir, but what—what about . . . ?"

"They can't be saved. They're dead now." Its voice rose. "Prepare to leave orbit, Mr. Farrell!"

"Yes, sir." Farrell's hand was moving toward a switch when the elevator opened. Kirk and McCoy stepped out of it. There were badly covered scratches on Kirk's face but the hand that held the phaser was steady. The double leaped from the command chair. "There's the impostor," it shouted. "Grab him!"

Nobody moved.

"You are the impostor," McCoy said.

"Don't believe him!" the double shrieked. "Take them both! Grab them!"

Kirk, McCoy beside him, walked on toward the command chair. Spock, reaching out a hand, halted McCoy, shaking his head. McCoy nodded—and Kirk moved on, alone.

"You want me dead, don't you? You want this ship all to yourself! But it's *mine!"*

Farrell had jumped from his chair. Spock touched his shoulder. "This is the Captain's private business," he said.

Kirk maintained his slow advance toward the maddened thing. It backed up, slow step by slow step, screaming.

"I am Captain Kirk, you ship of pigs! All right, let the liar destroy you all! He's already killed four of you! I run this ship! I own it. I own you—all of you!"

Kirk fired his phaser. The double crumpled to the deck, stunned.

"Spock, Bones," he said quietly. "Quickly, please."

Kirk had already taken up his position on the Transporter platform when they laid the unconscious body at his feet.

"You'll have to hold it, Captain," Spock said.

Kirk sat down on the platform. He lifted the drooping head to his shoulder, an arm around the flaccid waist. Then he looked up.

"Mr. Spock . . . "

"Yes, sir."

"If this doesn't work . . ."

"Understood, sir."

"Jim!" McCoy burst out. "Jim, don't do it! Not yet! In God's name, wait!"

"The console, Mr. Spock," Kirk said.

Spock's half-human part had taken him over. This could be good-bye to Kirk. At the console, he bowed his head over his treacherously shaking hands. When he lifted it, his face was calm, impassive.

"I am energizing, sir."

He saw Kirk draw the double closer to him. In the glow that lit the platform, he knew that he was seeing the embrace of an acknowledged, irrevocable brotherhood. Unfaltering, Spock reversed the console's controls. The hum of dematerialization rose. There was dazzle—and silence.

McCoy ran to the platform. Kirk stood on it, alone.

"Jim—Jim?" McCoy cried.

"Hello, Bones," Kirk said. He walked off the empty

platform and over to the console. "Mr. Spock," he said, "let's get those men of ours up and aboard."

Spock swallowed. "Yes, Captain. At once, sir."

It wasn't done at once. It was twenty minutes before the Transporter platform surrendered its burden of the four bodies to the eager hands awaiting them.

McCoy rose from his last examination. "They'll make it, Jim. Those rocks they heated saved their lives. They're all suffering from severe frostbite—but I think they'll make it."

The pallor of Kirk's face suddenly struck him. "How do *you* feel, Jim?"

There was a new sadness in Kirk's smile. "What's that old expression? 'Sadder but wiser.' I feel sadder, Bones, but much less wise."

"Join the human race, Jim," McCoy said.

There was a sense of quiet thanksgiving as Kirk entered the bridge. His first move was over to Spock at the computer station. "You know, of course," he said, "I could never have made it without you."

"Thank you, Captain. What do you plan to tell the crew?"

"The truth, Mr. Spock—that the impostor was put back where he belongs."

Janice Rand approached him. "I just wanted to say, Captain, how—glad I am that . . . "

"Thank you, Yeoman." Kirk returned to his command chair. The girl watched him go. Spock watched the girl.

"That impostor," he said, "had some very interesting qualities. And he certainly resembled the Captain. You agree, I'm sure, Yeoman Rand."

She had flushed scarlet. But she met his quizzical eyes with courage. "Yes, Mr. Spock. The impostor had some exceedingly interesting qualities."

CATSPAW

(Robert Bloch)

The persistent static crackling from Lieutenant Uhura's communications panel was just the minor worry presented by the planet Pyris VII. A dark and forbidding star it had shown itself to be ever since the *Enterprise* had entered its orbit—a chunk of black granite hurled into space to no ostensible purpose, lightless, lifeless except for members of the Starship's landing party beamed down to it for routine investigation and check-in reports. That was the big worry—the absence of any check-in reports. Yet Scott, Sulu and crewman Jackson were all aware of standard landing-group procedure. They knew it required an hourly check-in from any team assigned to explore an unknown planet.

Uhura looked up at Kirk. "Still no response, sir."

"Keep it open."

He frowned at another burst of static from the communications panel. "I don't like this. Nothing since the first check-in. Scott and Sulu should have contacted us half an hour ago."

Spock said, "Perhaps they have nothing to report. Though Pyris VII is a Class M planet capable of sustaining humanoid life, our own people are the only evidence of it our sensors have been able to pick up."

"Nevertheless, Scott and Sulu are obliged to check in, regardless of whether they have anything official to report. Why don't they answer?"

Uhura adjusted a control. A look of relief came into her face. "Contact established, Captain."

Kirk seized the audio. Jackson's voice said, "Jackson to *Enterprise*."

"Kirk here."

"One to beam up, sir."

60

"One? Jackson, where are Scott and Sulu?"

"I'm ready to beam up, sir."

"Jackson! Where are—" A roar of static overwhelmed his words. Uhura tried to control it; and failed. "I'm sorry, sir. I can't clear it."

"All right," said Kirk. "Notify Transporter Room to prepare to beam up one member of the landing party. Have Dr. McCoy report to me in Transporter Room on the double."

"Yes, sir."

It was the measure of their anxiety that Kirk and Spock both ran for the elevator. They opened the door of the Transporter Room to the steady, throbbing hum of thrown switches.

"Ready, sir," the technician said.

"Energize!" The humming rose to a keening pitch and McCoy hurried in with his medikit.

"What's on, Jim?"

"Trouble."

The Transporter platform glowed into dazzle. Then its sparkle gathered into the full figure of crewman Jackson. He stood, stiff and unmoving, his face wiped clean of all expression, his eyes unseeing, fixed in a glassy stare. The hum of materialization faded. Kirk strode to the platform. "Jackson! What happened? Where are the others?"

The mouth moved as though preparing to speak. But Jackson didn't speak. The mouth twisted into a grimace—and Jackson, pitching forward, toppled to the floor.

Kneeling beside him, McCoy looked up at Kirk. He shook his head. "The man's dead, Jim."

Kirk stared down at the body. Its glassy eyes were still fixed on nothing. Then, horribly, the jaw dropped and the mouth opened. Out of it spoke a voice, deep, harsh, guttural. "Captain Kirk, you hear me. There is a curse on your ship. Leave this star. It is death that waits for you here . . . "

There was a moment of appalled stillness. Jackson's dead mouth still yawned open. But his lips had not moved.

At his desk in Sickbay, McCoy leaned his head on his hand. He didn't look up as Kirk opened the door. Shoulders sagged, he pushed wearily at a heap of tape cartridges in front of him.

"Well?" Kirk said.

McCoy lifted a handful of the cartridges. Then he dropped them. "These are the reports of every test I've run. There's no sign of any injury, none. No organic damage, internal or external."

Kirk was silent for a stretched moment. Scott and Sulu—they were still down there on the planet that had returned a dead man to the *Enterprise*; a dead man whose mouth had been used by that awful voice. "*Then why is Jackson dead, Bones?*"

"He froze to death," McCoy said.

Spock had quietly joined them. "That doesn't seem reasonable, Doctor," he said. "The climate of Pyris VII approximates that of Earth's central Western hemisphere during the summer solstice."

McCoy said irritably, "I know that, Spock. But reasonable or unreasonable, Jackson froze to death. He was literally dead on his feet when he materialized in the Transporter Room."

"He was about to speak," Kirk said.

"He was dead, I tell you!" McCoy shouted.

"Someone spoke." Kirk slowly shook his head. "There seems to be a good deal more to that planet than our sensors have been able to detect! With Scott and Sulu virtually marooned down there . . ."

He was interrupted by the buzzing intercom on McCoy's desk. He hit the switch. "Kirk here."

Uhura, her voice urgent, said, "Sir, we've lost all traces of Mr. Scott and Mr. Sulu. The sensors no longer register any indication of life on the planet's surface. That's Mr. Farrell's last report."

"Well," said Kirk, "that tears it." He paused. "Thank you, Lieutenant. Have Mr. Farrell maintain sensor scan." He snapped off the intercom. "Spock, Bones, get your gear together for a landing party. We're beaming down to find them."

Fog was what they found. Clammy swirls of it drifted around them as they materialized on a twilight world of rock, barren, desolate. From the craggy knoll they stood on, no green was visible—just a gray vista of mist that moved sluggishly, only to reveal more mist, more rock, black fields, black hills of rock.

"Odd," Kirk said. "Our probe data didn't indicate fog."

"Odd, indeed," Spock agreed. "No bodies of water. No cloud formations. No variations in surface temperature. Under such conditions, fog is impossible." He had unslung his tricorder and was taking readings.

"It was impossible for Jackson to freeze to death in this climate," McCoy said. "Yet that's what happened. By the way, just where are we?"

"According to Transporter Room coordinates, this is the exact spot from which Jackson was beamed up to the ship," Spock said.

"Readings, Mr. Spock?"

"No indication of—wait! I'm picking up a life forms reading at 14 degrees mark 7—distance 137.16 meters." He looked up from the tricorder. "Multiple readings, Captain!"

Astonished, Kirk snapped on his communicator. "Kirk to *Enterprise*."

Static distorted Uhura's voice. "*Enterprise*, Captain."

"How do the ship's sensors read now, Lieutenant?"

"All we're getting are physical impulses from you, Mr. Spock and Dr. McCoy, sir. There's nothing else alive down there."

The static almost obliterated her last words. "I can hardly hear you, Lieutenant," Kirk said. "Can you hear me?"

His communicator cracked with a crash of static. Disgusted, Kirk snapped it off and was returning it to his belt when McCoy said, "The fog's getting thicker. Maybe it accounts for the interference."

It *was* getting thicker. Fog rolled around them so dense now that they could scarcely see each other. "There has to be some explanation for the disparity in the readings," Kirk said. "Ours are the only life forms picked up by the ship's sensors but Spock's tricorder registers multiple forms. Do your readings still hold, Mr. Spock?"

"No change, sir."

"Phasers on the ready," Kirk said.

Then they all heard it—a high-pitched wailing. Faint at first, it grew in volume to a mournful shrieking. "They must have heard us," McCoy whispered.

"Quiet, Bones!"

McCoy gripped Kirk's arm as he pointed with the other hand. Ahead of them the coiling fog had begun to glow with a greenish, sickly luminescence. Then it gathered, shaping itself into three cloudy faces, vaguely featured, indistinct, wrinkled by a hundred years. Elf locks of wispy white hair hung about them, their sex as blurred as their features. One of the faces spoke.

"Captain Kirk . . . "

Its long-drawn-out whine had the same creepy cadence as the wailing.

Kirk stepped forward. "Who are you?"

"Go baaack—" wailed the toothless mouth.

The mist was sending the bodiless faces in and out of focus.

"Winds shall rise," one of them whimpered

"And fogs descend . . . "

"Death is here . . . "

On a cackle of rheumy laughter, the faces suddenly came apart. Then they dissolved into mist.

Quiet, unmoved, Spock said, "Illusion, Captain." He lowered his tricorder. "They contained neither physical substance nor energy. It may have been a projection of some sort."

"Shakespeare wrote of a blasted heath," Kirk said. "And of warning witches. But why should these have appeared to us? None of us care to become the King of Scotland. Spock, did the life form readings change during that little encounter?"

"They remained the same, Captain."

Kirk nodded. "That may be part of our answer."

They moved on—and an abrupt gust of wind whistled past them. It grew stronger. It should have tattered the fog into shreds. It didn't. The stuff became clammier, more blinding. The wind now rose to a gale force that compelled them to turn their backs to it, clinging to each other for support. "Hang on!" Kirk shouted. As though the words were some form of exorcism, the wind was gone as suddeny as it had come.

Panting, McCoy said, "That was one very realistic illusion." He drew a deep lungful of breath. Then, incredulously, he whispered, "Jim—ahead of us—there . . ."

It looked like the keep of a medieval castle. It reared itself up before them, huge, battlemented, its masonry of massive stones hoary with age. Its great oaken door, beamed and iron-bound, was slightly ajar. On one of the worn steps that led up to it crouched a sleek black cat. A glittering gold chain was hung around its neck. As they approached it, they saw that a translucent crystal pendant was attached to the chain. The pose of the cat suggested it was waiting for something. Mice, perhaps.

Spock said, "This is the source of the life forms reading, Captain. They are inside somewhere."

Kirk tried to use his communicator again, only to be defeated by an explosion of static. Once more he hung it back on his belt.

"Is this how we lost contact with the first landing party?" McCoy wondered.

"What about that, Spock?" Kirk put it to him. "Does this apparent castle have anything to do with the static?"

The Vulcan consulted his tricorder. "I would say not, sir. There's no evidence of anything that would directly cause the interference. Both the castle and the cat are equally real."

"Or unreal," Kirk said. "Some illusions can manifest themselves in solid substance. Why didn't our sensors pick up this castle? And why didn't they register the life forms inside it?" He looked up, frowning, at a turreted wall. "It could be exerting a force field that has cut off our sensor scan."

"Then it would also affect Spock's tricorder, wouldn't it?" McCoy asked.

"Would it? I'm beginning to wonder—" It was as Kirk spoke the last words that the cat mewed, rose gracefully and disappeared through the partly open door. Lost, it seemed, in some private speculation, he watched it go. Then pulling himself out of it briskly, "Well," he said, "if Scott and Sulu are anywhere around, this is the most likely place. Come on."

Phasers in hand, they pushed the door open. A squeaking shrilled over their heads—and a cloud of bats swooped through the door, chittering, their leathery wings almost brushing their faces.

Ducking, McCoy cried, "What the devil was that?"

"*Desmodus rufus*," Spock said. "Vampire bats."

"That's an Earth species," Kirk said. The cat, moving restlessly before them, mewed again as it turned into the darkness beyond the doorway. He looked after it, the look of private thoughtfulness back on his face. "And so is the cat an Earth species. The plot thickens. Castles, black cats, vampire bats and witches. If we weren't missing two live officers and a dead crewman, I'd say someone was putting on an elaborate Halloween trick or treat."

"Trick or treat, Captain?"

"An old Earth custom, Mr. Spock. Explanation later."

The castle walls appeared to be hewn from solid rock. The cat padded silently ahead of Kirk as he and the others groped along the chilly corridor. It was dim, its uncertain light provided by occasional torches whose flames flared and ebbed above their iron sconces, cobwebbed and rusty.

"Dust. Cobwebs. Halloween is right," McCoy said.

The cat slipped around a corner into a darker corner. As they followed, the floor gave way beneath them, and they were plunged into blackness.

Kirk was the first to recover his senses. Someone with a bizarre sense of humor had arranged to place a spiked Iron Maiden right before him. The skull of the human skeleton inside it grinned at him. He refused to be horrified. What concerned him was the discovery that he was shackled to the dungeon's wall. So were Spock and McCoy. Then he realized that all their equipment—phasers, communicators, tricorders—had been removed.

"Mr. Spock . . ."

The Vulcan stirred in his fetters. "I am undamaged, Captain."

"Is Bones all right?"

McCoy spoke for himself. "Nothing broken—just a lot of bruises. What was that you said about trick or treat, Jim?"

"Curses, dungeons, Iron Maidens, skeletons. The point is, these are all Earth manifestations. *Why?*"

"The tricorder registered this castle as real, Jim." McCoy rattled his chains. "And *these* are no illusion. This place could be an Earth parallel."

"But it would be a parallel only of Earth superstition, Doctor," Spock said. "Something that exists only in the minds of men."

"Exactly," Kirk said. "It's as though—" He broke off. Muffled footsteps had sounded from the corridor outside. A key scraped in the dungeon's lock; to Kirk's astounded relief, its heavy door was swung open by Scott and Sulu.

"Scotty! Sulu! You're safe!"

There was no sign of responsive joy on either of their faces. Silent, stone-faced, Scott pulled a phaser from his belt—and leveled it at them.

"Scotty," Kirk said, "put that phaser down!"

Unmoving, unblinking, Scott maintained the phaser at aim.

"*Scott!*" Kirk shouted.

"Jim, I think they've been drugged. Look at their eyes—no nictation. They don't blink at all."

"Neither did Jackson," Spock said.

"These two are alive! Scotty, Sulu—do you know who I am?"

Sulu nodded.

"What's happened to you?" Kirk demanded.

For answer, Sulu shuffled past him to lean over McCoy. While Scott covered the *Enterprise* physician with the phaser, Sulu selected a key from a bunch he was carrying on a ring, and inserted it in the bolt's lock that bound the chains to McCoy's arms. Watching, Kirk said, "They're just taking off the chains, Bones. They're not going to let us go. Are you?"

Silence. In absolute silence, their manacles were unlocked. At the dungeon door, Sulu motioned them into the corridor. Gauging Scott's distance behind him, Kirk whirled around to throw a punch at his jaw. The butt of the phaser caught him in the temple. As he stumbled to his knees, Spock jumped Scott and McCoy made a leap for the unarmed Sulu. But even as they touched them, their faces were lit by the sickly greenish light—and they dissolved into it.

"*Stop!*"

It was the voice that had spoken through the dead mouth of Jackson.

They stopped. The green glow seemed to have dissolved the corridor and the dungeon, too. All that was familiar was the strangeness of Scott and Sulu. They had reappeared, as unblinking, as blank-faced as before. Everything else was new.

And old. The large chamber to which they'd somehow been transported was heavy with medieval magnificence. Dark tapestries covered its walls. The flare of its sconced torches shone on the bare surface of a huge table, flanked by high-backed chairs. But Kirk's eyes had fixed on a man. He sat on an ornately carved chair, set on a dais that was canopied by a domelike structure. He was bearded, and the long robe he wore glittered with the gold-embroidered symbols of the Zodiac. The black wand he held was topped by a dazzling crystal ball. The cat was stretched out at his feet.

Kirk strode up to the chair. "Whoever you are, you've proved your skill at creating illusions. Now what I want to know is what you have done to my men."

The man leaned forward. "Your race owns a ridiculous predilection for resistance. You question everything. Is it not sufficient for you to *accept* what is?"

"Not when one of my men is dead and two others have been turned into mindless . . . "

"Not mindless, Captain Kirk. The live ones are merely—controlled."

Spock and McCoy had made startled movements at the man's use of Kirk's name. They were noted. "Yes, we know you, all of you. Don't we, my precious?" He lowered a hand to stroke the cat.

"Who are you?" Kirk demanded. "Why did you bring us here?"

The bearded mouth smiled. "My name is Korob. As for bringing you here, you insisted upon coming. You were warned away from here."

"For what reason?" Kirk waved a hand that embraced all the mystic trappings of the room and the man. "What is all this—farce about?"

"Farce? I assure you, it is not that, Captain."

Spock spoke. "Clearly, you are unfamiliar with your planet, Korob."

The piercing eyes searched the Vulcan's face. "What did you say?"

"No life exists on your planet," Spock said. "Mapping expeditions have charted this solar system. Their scientific surveys prove that no life forms have ever lived where you appear to live."

The cat stirred, mewing. Lids lowered over the piercing eyes. "That we are not native to this planet is of no importance," Korob said softly.

"It's important to the Federation," Kirk said. "What are you doing here?"

"All in good time, Captain." The cat mewed again, and Korob bent his head as though listening to a secret message. When he raised it, he said, "You must forgive me. I have been an inattentive host. You will join me in something with which to refresh yourselves." Followed by the cat, he rose to lead the way toward the empty table.

"That cat—" McCoy said quietly.

"Yes," Spock said. "It reminds me of certain ancient Earth legends concerning wizards and their 'familiars'— demons in animal form sent by Satan to serve the wizards."

"Superstition," Kirk said.

"I did not create the legends, Captain. I merely repeat them."

Korob turned. "You are the different one, Mr. Spock. There are no colors in your patterns of logic. You think only in terms of black and white. You see all this around you. Yet you do not believe in it."

"He doesn't know about trick or treat," McCoy said.

Korob smiled faintly. "I see." He waved toward the empty table. "But, gentlemen, please join me at dinner."

Nobody moved. Scott and Sulu made a menacing move, Scott lifting the phaser. Korob held up his hand. They both backed up to stand stock-still again. "I had hoped you would be more flexible," Korob said, "but—" He raised his wand.

The green glow grew into a dazzle, dazzling as the crystal ball on the wand's end. The room and all its objects spun in it like dust motes. It blinded Kirk. When he could see again, he, Spock and McCoy were seated at the table. A boar's head gaped in front of him. There was a platter of stuffed peacock. In the table's center a giant beef roast, browned to succulence, was surrounded by silver bowls of fruit, great plates of creamy cheeses. Massive candelabra refracted light on crystal wine decanters and golden goblets. As a display of medieval food and sumptuous service, it was a feast to be seen only by tourists who had booked passage in a Time Machine.

"How in the name of—" McCoy began.

"Not a trick, Doctor," Korob said. "A treat this time. Believe that."

"What do you want from us, Korob?" Kirk asked.

"For the moment, merely that you eat and enjoy yourselves. Please try the wine, Doctor. You will find it excellent."

"No, thank you," McCoy said.

Mewing, the cat suddenly leaped to an empty seat at the table, light glinting from the crystal pendant hung around its neck. Despite his refusal of wine, McCoy's hand reached for the decanter in front of him. He made a visible effort to pull it back—and failed. Kirk made a move toward him only to be slammed back in his chair by Scott.

"Bones . . . "

"He can't obey you, Captain," Korob said. "He will not be harmed."

Will paralyzed, McCoy poured wine from the decanter into his goblet. The cat, its crystal pendant shining against its black fur, watched steadily as he raised the goblet to his lips. He touched it with them—and the wine burst into vivid red flames.

Clearly alarmed, Korob raised his wand. The flames subsided, and McCoy dashed the goblet to the floor. It vanished, leaving a smell of smoke in the air.

The cat hissed.

Furious, Kirk said, "If you've amused yourself sufficiently, Korob . . . "

But Korob's eyes were on the cat. "That was not my wish," he said. "I—perhaps I can make proper amends."

The black wand pointed to the table's empty plates. They filled with gems, pricelessly exotic jewels come together in their multicolored glitter from the multiworlds of the galaxy—the ruby reds of what were not rubies, the sapphire blues of what were not sapphires but the alien treasures of an unearthly star system.

"They look genuine," McCoy said.

"They are, I assure you," Korob said. "That is a masgar, Doctor—a lorinium—a pavonite. There is a fortune for each of you in the richest gems of the galaxy if you will leave here without further query."

"We are not ready to leave here," Kirk said quietly.

"Captain, you are a stubborn and unreasonable man. However, you have passed the tests."

"Tests?" McCoy queried.

Korob nodded. "You proved your loyalty by coming here to rescue your comrades in spite of warnings to stay away. Your courage was also tested. I learned you couldn't be frightened. Now I've learned that you can't be bribed. I congratulate you."

The cat mewed. Korob patted it. "Quite right," he said. "Go at once." The animal jumped from the chair and was gone through the tapestried archway at the other end of the chamber.

Kirk got up. "All right. Now that you've tested our integrity, suppose you demonstrate yours."

"Gladly, Captain."

"Begin by explaining what you've done to Scott and Sulu. How are you 'controlling' them?"

"I cannot answer that question," Korob said. "But I have sent for someone who can."

That someone entered, a tall, slim woman. Her black hair, parted in the center above her acquiline features, fell below her waist. Perhaps it was her high cheekbones that gave her green eyes an oblique look. On the breast of her red gown she wore a crystal pendant like the one they had seen on the cat.

Korob said, "This is my colleague, Sylvia."

As she approached Kirk, he became conscious of her remarkable grace. Bowing slightly, she said, "Captain Kirk, I understand you want to know what we did to your men. We probed their minds. For us it is a simple matter to probe the minds of creatures like yourself."

"Hypnosis?" Spock asked.

She ignored him to move to McCoy. As she did so, she said, "Our methods go a little deeper than hypnosis." McCoy made no comment. Eyes held by the glowing pendant, he had gone suddenly rigid, unblinking. She smiled at him. "Let me tell you what you said of the man Jackson who was returned to your ship. You said, 'There's no sign of any injury ... no organic damage, internal or external. The man simply froze to death.' "

"How do you know that?" Kirk was watching her closely.

The green eyes turned to him. "You like to think of yourselves as complex creatures, Captain, but you are flawed. Your minds have many doors. Most of them are left unguarded. We enter your minds through those unguarded doors."

"Telepathy?" Spock suggested.

This time she answered him. "Not entirely. Telepathy does not include control. And I assure you, I am in full control of your friends."

Abruptly, Kirk lost patience with the charming lady and her conversation. Moving swiftly, he shoved his heavy chair back into Scott. Scott stumbled, losing his guard stance behind the chair. He lost his phaser, too; Kirk grabbed it from him all in that same swift, unexpected movement. Scott, recovering his balance, lunged. Kirk leveled the phaser at him. He backed up, and the phaser swung around to cover all of them— Sylvia, Korob, Sulu, Scott.

"Don't move—any of you!" Kirk said.

McCoy relaxed. His eyes blinked. Kirk motioned Scott and Sulu over to Korob, the phaser steady in his hand. "No more hocus-pocus!" he said. "Korob, I want our other weapons and our equipment. I want them now. I also want some answers—real ones."

Sylvia said, "Put that weapon down, Captain."

Kirk laughed. The green eyes didn't flash with anger. They merely regarded him appraisingly. Then, reaching a hand into a pocket slit in her gown, Sylvia withdrew from it what appeared to be a small silver toy. She left Kirk to go to Spock and McCoy.

"Do you recognize this?" she asked them.

"It looks like a miniature model of the *Enterprise*," McCoy said.

"No. In a sense it *is* the *Enterprise*."

Frowning, Spock said, "Where did you get it?"

"From the minds of your two crew memebers. I absorbed their knowledge of the ship."

"With what purpose in *your* mind?" Spock asked.

She moved to the table where the huge candelabra held its tall, lit candles. "In the mythology of your race," she said, "this is called 'sympathetic magic,' Captain. One may call it what one chooses. It is an interesting tool."

Kirk, still holding the phaser on Korob, spoke over his shoulder. "Lady," he said, "that won't do as a explanation."

Spock's face had grown grave. He watched her intently as she stood at the table, the candlelight throwing come-and-go shadows across her face. "Jackson," she said, "you all wondered why he froze to death in a moderate climate. How is *this* explanation, Captain? I made an exact image of him. Then I froze the image. When I knew it was frozen, he died."

"Rubbish!" Kirk said. "You can't *think* a man to death!"

"Your communicator is in the pocket of Korob's robe, Captain. Please take it."

He hesitated a moment before he obeyed. As he turned, he saw that she was holding the toy model of

Enterprise about six inches above a candle flame. "Signal your ship," she said.

He clicked the communicator open. Uneasy in spite of himself, he realized that she had lowered the silver model closer to the candle flame.

Korob said, "Sylvia—don't . . . "

The model sank closer to the candle flame; and Kirk spoke hastily into the communicator. "Kirk to *Enterprise! Enterprise*, come in, please. Kirk here. Come in . . . "

"Captain, it's you!" It was Uhura's voice but there was desperation in it. "Where are you? We can't . . ."

"Never mind us. What's happening up there?"

"Something's—gone wrong with the temperature control. We—can't locate it. The heat has risen—sixty degrees in the past thirty seconds. The *Enterprise* is burning up, sir . . . "

"Beef up the refrigerator units, Lieutenant!"

The voice came more weakly now. "We did, sir— but they're—breaking down . . . "

Kirk, visualizing his Starship, saw it streaking through space like a comet on fire. He imagined Uhura and Farrell, hanging onto their posts, gasping for air, their uniforms sweat-drenched. "The heat will go," he said. "I'll take care of it, Lieutenant."

He snapped off the communicator, walked over to Korob and returned it to him. "All right," he told Sylvia. "You can stop it now." He handed the phaser, too, to Korob.

She removed the little ship from the flame.

"Now that you've seen our science," Korob said, "perhaps you'd better tell us something of yours."

"I'd rather know more about yours," Kirk said. "First you call it magic. Now it's science. Which is it?"

"What would you call it, Captain?"

"Transmutation—telekinesis. You seem to have a strange ability, not just to change the molecular structure of objects, but to move them from point to point by merely willing it. What could you want with our comparatively clumsy science?"

"Ours requires machines, matter, energy, chemicals," Spock added. "Compared with your techniques, it is imperfect and cumbersome. Then why is it important to you?"

"There are things you know that we do not. We can alter the molecular structure of matter. But you can release the energy within it."

"Korob! You talk too much!" Sylvia snapped. Recovering herself, she went on, "Besides, you three are not so specialized as those two." She indicated the motionless figures of Scott and Sulu. "That one thinks only of machines. The other's mind is full of trivia, thoughts about his collections, the physical exertions he calls exercises. But in your minds is an accumulated knowledge of worlds, of this galaxy."

"If so, in our minds is where the knowledge stays," Kirk said.

"You have used Scott and Sulu as catspaws," McCoy said. "You used them to lure us down here. How did you know we'd come?"

"*They* knew you'd come," Korob smiled.

"Enough of this," Sylvia said impatiently. "You will tell us what we want to know, one way or another!"

"It's a little late for threats," Kirk said. "I contacted my ship, remember? How long do you think it'll be before there's another landing party here?"

"Quite some time," Korob said. He touched the tiny ship on the table with the crystal ball of his wand. The now familiar greenish light glowed over it. When it faded, the model was encased in a solid block of crystal. "An impenetrable force field now surrounds your ship, Captain. It will not hinder orbit. It does, however, make prisoners of everybody inside your ship."

"I advise you to cooperate, Captain," Sylvia said. "Though it is simple to extract the information we want by forcible means, they are extremely painful. And they have a certain—draining effect." She waved a hand toward Scott and Sulu.

"We have nothing to discuss," Kirk said.

Korob turned to Scott and Sulu. "Take them back to their cell."

"Wait." Sylvia's green eyes moved over them, cold, icily analytical. "The Doctor will stay."

"Bones—" Kirk began.

"Don't waste your sympathy, Captain. You will be next. It really makes little difference." She turned, speaking sharply to Scott and Sulu. "Take the others away."

Korob handed Sulu the phaser. It thrust hard into Kirk's back as he and Spock were herded from the chamber.

This time his shackles seemed tighter to Kirk. His eyes fixed anxiously on the dungeon door, he moved restlessly in the chains, feeling them grind into his flesh.

"How long has it been?" he fretted.

"Twenty-two minutes, seventeen seconds," Spock said.

The question gnawing at Kirk burst out of him. "What are they doing to him?"

"Perhaps," Spock said, "the real question is 'what are they?' They've admitted they are alien to this planet. And I find their total ignorance of our instrumentality and science most curious."

Kirk gave him an interested glance. "They also refer to us as 'creatures,' as though our species were unfamiliar to them."

Spock nodded. "The fact that everything around us seems solid and real may not be the fact. Sylvia and Korob look humanoid. But they fabricated that food and the gems. They may also have fabricated the way they appear to us. Suppose they are not biped humanoids? Suppose they've just drawn all this from the subconscious minds of Scott and Sulu?"

Kirk frowned. "Scotty and Sulu are responsible men. They are not prone to superstition." He paused to digest Spock's speculations. "But Scott, it's true, does *have* a heritage that includes castles, dungeons and witches in its lore. And Sulu—Oriental folk tales also admit the influence of ghosts and spirits."

"Children are still fond of ghost stories, Captain. Even I grew up with a knowledge of them, much to my father's dismay. Perhaps we are all subconsciously afraid of dark rooms, of spectral visions—and this is what these aliens are using to try and gain the information they want."

"But they don't want just our science," Kirk reminded him. "What they're after is knowledge about our worlds—the galaxy itself." He was about to add *"Why?"* when the key scraped in the lock of the dungeon's door.

It opened. Sulu, phaser in hand, pushed McCoy through it. He didn't resist the shove. He just stood there, unblinking, his face emptied of all human expression.

"Ah, Bones, Bones—" Kirk groaned.

But Sulu had bent over him and was unlocking his chains. Then McCoy shambled over to him. He jerked Kirk to his feet, and placing him carefully in line with Sulu's pointed phaser, kicked him toward the open dungeon door.

Sylvia's method for making an obedient imbecile out of McCoy had disturbed Korob. As they awaited Kirk's arrival in the castle's great hall, he put his agitation into words.

"There's no need to torture them!"

"They resist," she said.

"You tease them! You promise them toys and then watch them scream in pain when they reach out to touch them. It amuses you!"

She shrugged. "And if it does, that does not concern you. I get the information I want for the Old Ones; and to get it is why we were sent here."

"You must *stop!*" Korob cried. "At least, let the pain be brief!"

"You cannot command me, Korob. We are equals."

"But not the same," he said.

"No. You are weak. I am strong. That is the reason I was chosen by the Old Ones to come with you. They suspect you of weakness. I am the one they—" She stopped at the appearance of Kirk between McCoy and Sulu.

Her lips moved into a charming smile. In the voice of a hostess greeting a distinguished guest, she said, "Captain, how nice to see you. I'm so glad you have come." The welcoming smile still on her mouth, she turned to Korob. "Leave us—and take those two with you."

Korob hesitated. Then, making Sylvia a formal bow, he picked up the *Enterprise* in its transparent casing— and left the chamber, followed by the listless Sulu and McCoy.

Kirk and Sylvia eyed each other. For the first time he sensed tension in her, a certain wariness as though she knew she'd met her match in strength. The smile he gave her was just as charming as the one that still lingered on her face. "What now?" he said pleasantly. "Do you wave your magic wand and destroy my mind, too?"

He didn't miss the involuntary start she gave at mention of the wand. He also noted how her hand had lifted to touch the crystal pendant on her breast. "There's no real damage done to the mind, Captain— just a drain of knowledge and will."

"You don't call that damage?"

"Why should I when it isn't?" she responded easily.

His eyes swept over her in the immemorial look of the sexually appraising male. "You must forgive me," he said. "I forget that you are not a woman. Perhaps not even human."

"I don't know what you mean," she said.

"All this—" he waved his hand around the room, "all this apparently drawn from our racial superstitions and fantasies. Illusion—the whole thing."

She pointed to one of the wall torches. "Put your hand in that flame and you will be burned, Captain. However created, these things are quite real. I am real, too."

"Why do you need us?" he said.

She walked over to the table. When she turned to face him again, she said, "What does your science teach you about the nature of the universe?"

He laughed. "There's nothing I enjoy so much as discussions on the nature of the universe. Particularly with charming ladies." He gave her a mocking little bow. "You didn't answer my question, you know. Why do you need us?"

"I don't need the others. Nor do you."

She spoke softly. Now she left the table to move closer to him. Human or not, she *was* graceful. "If we combined what you know and I know," she said, "there's no limit to the power we would possess."

"And Korob?" he said.

One thing she *did* know, he was thinking—how to exert sexual witchcraft. She'd laid her hand lightly, very lightly on his forearm. "Korob is a weak and foolish man," she said. "He can be disposed of. But I would find it difficult to dispose of—you."

He smiled down into the green eyes. "Or to probe my mind?"

"That would not be necessary if we mingled our knowledge," she said. "From me you could learn secrets you've never dreamed of. Anything you imagined could be yours . . ."

The hand was slowly moving up his arm. "Your—arguments are quite persuasive," he said. "Suppose I decided to go along with you?"

Her low murmur was a caress. "You would not regret your decision. Power, wealth, all the luxuries of your galaxy would be yours."

"You're a very beautiful woman," he said—and meant it.

"I can be many beautiful women," she said. The green eyes upturned to his were suddenly sapphire blue. The long black hair disappeared and became a shining tumble of blond curls. Even her red robe drained of its color to change into a creamy white that matched the flawless cream of her skin. Then the blond beauty was gone. Copper braids wreathed her head. The robe deepened to a rich bronze. She was an autumn beauty now, her cheeks flushed with the tone of autumn leaves.

"Do you like me thus?" she asked. "Or do you prefer this?"

She recovered her original appearance.

"I prefer this," Kirk said—and took her in his arms. When she lifted her head from his kiss, she was staring at him with surprised delight. "That was very—enjoyable. What is it called? May I have another?"

He kissed her again. Then he released her. "Your people will guarantee me that I won't be harmed?"

"Yes, when they come. I have only to report to the Old Ones that you will cooperate with us."

"And my friends will be restored to their former condition?"

"Of course—if you wish it."

She reached up her arms to his neck but he removed them.

"What's wrong? What wrong have I done?"

He stepped away from her. "When you took the form of a woman," he said, "you also assumed the female compulsion to talk too much. You've revealed too many secrets, Sylvia. What if your Old Ones find out you've been tricked by one of the creatures you plan to conquer?"

"You tricked me? You do not like me?"

"No," he said.

"Then you just used me?"

"Didn't you plan to use me?"

Her green eyes blazed. She clapped her hands sharply. Scott and McCoy, both armed with phasers, came through the tapestried archway.

She pointed a shaking, sharp-nailed finger at Kirk. "Get him out of here! Take him back to his cell!"

It was Korob who came to release him from his shackles.

But in spite of the phaser in his hand, he seemed hurried, anxious. Kirk and Spock watched him in tense silence as he unlocked their chains. To their astonishment, they were no sooner freed than he handed Kirk the phaser and pulled the communicator from his robe's pocket.

He spoke in a whisper. "I have broken the crystal that imprisoned the model of your ship, Captain. It was time. Your people had found a way to break out of the force field. It is difficult to control so many things. You must go now before she discovers the weapon is missing."

"We can't leave without our men," Kirk said.

Korob made an impatient gesture. "They are not

your men any longer. They belong to Sylvia. I can no longer control them—or her."

He glanced fearfully at the dungeon door. "There was no need for any of this. We could have entered your galaxy in peace. But Sylvia is not content with conquest. She is close to the Old Ones and she wants to destroy."

"You came in a ship?" Spock asked.

Korob shook his head. "We used a power pack." He motioned to the door. "There's no time to explain now. We must go. She plans to kill us all."

Kirk and Spock had started to follow him to the door when Korob suddenly turned, stopping them with a warning gesture. They both heard it at the same time— the sound of a deep, resonant purr. Then through the open door of the cell they saw the shadow; the creeping shadow of a great cat silhouetted against the farther wall of the corridor.

"Keep back," Korob muttered.

He drew his wand from his robe. Holding it poised, he slid into the corridor toward the cat's shadow. But already it had begun to grow in size and was looming black, gigantic against the corridor wall. And the purr had changed. Ferocity had entered into its deep growl. Snarling, the cat now towered over a Korob whose face had convulsed with terror. He lifted his wand, shouting, "No, no—get back! *No!*"

The shadow lifted a monstrous paw. Korob screamed, crumpled, the wand falling from his hand. Kirk and Spock ran to reach him. There was an animal roar of rage as the huge paw lifted again. Kirk had barely time to seize the wand before Spock grabbed him—and slammed the dungeon door closed behind them.

A latch on its outside clanked into its slot. They were locked into the cell again.

Its door shook as some immense body pushed against it. Maddened roars rebounded in echoes from the corridor as the unseen monster-cat hurled itself against the door again. Spock shouted, "It won't hold long against such pressure, sir!"

"Move back," Kirk said. He aimed the phaser at the

door and fired. There was no effect. "It's out of energy," he said, examining the weapon. "She must have drained it. We could have jumped Scott or Sulu any time—and we never knew it." He glanced around the cell. "There's no way out of here."

"Only one," Spock said. "The way we got in."

Another thud shook the door. Kirk said, "This wall's too smooth to climb."

Spock had his eyes on the trapdoor above his head. "If you were to boost me up, sir, I could pull you up from there."

"It's a good eight feet. Think you can make it?"

"Ready when you are, Captain."

Kirk nodded, laid the wand on the floor, and bending his back, braced himself on spread legs as Spock climbed up on his shoulders. The Vulcan got his grip on the trapdoor opening. He hauled himself up through it, and Kirk, retrieving the wand, reached for the hand Spock extended down to him. As he found his own grip on the opening, the cell door crashed down. The cat's head, lips drawn back over its teeth, filled the empty space. It opened its jaws in a scream of rage.

Breathless, Kirk said, "That's what I call a close thing. Where are McCoy and the others?"

"Maybe we should return with weapons and another landing party, Captain."

"I'm not leaving them here," Kirk said. He moved on, and was leading the way along the dimly lit passage when Spock paused. "I don't think this is the way we came, Captain."

"Maybe, maybe not," Kirk said. "It's like a maze in here. Look, there's a turn ahead there. And we *did* come around a turn . . ."

Perhaps it was a sound, not a sixth sense that warned him. He whirled just in time to avoid a blow by the mace McCoy held in both hands. As it struck the wall with a shattering clang, Scott darted from the shadowy angle of the corridor to lift a mace above Spock's head. Spock ducked its swoop and closed with Scott, applying his Vulcan neck-pinch. It felled Scott who dropped his weapon. Spock simultaneously shouted, "Behind you, sir!"

Kirk had just toppled McCoy with a punch to the jaw. Now he wheeled, to be smashed against the wall by Sulu's booted foot. He grabbed it and brought Sulu crashing down on top of him, knocked out.

He looked up at Spock. "You were right. We *did* take the wrong turn—but at least we found them."

"I'd hardly call it that, Captain. But now that we do have them all together . . . "

The snarling roar sounded very close. The shadow of the immense cat grew blacker and blacker on the corridor wall. Its claws were extending from one enormous paw.

Kirk lifted the wand. "This," he said, "is your 'power pack,' isn't it, Sylvia?"

The cat's shadow vanished. Sylvia, dark-haired, red-robed, stood against the wall.

Kirk fingered the wand. "This crystal—and the one you wear—both serve as the source of your power, don't they?"

"The source? No, Captain, the mind is the wellspring of our power. My crystal is merely an amplifier. The wand controls much more."

"With such power at your command, what did you want of us?" Spock asked her.

"I have wanted nothing of you, Mr. Spock. Your mind is a deep well of facts. It is the people of Earth I wanted. Their minds are the deep wells of dreams—the material we need to create our realities."

"You consume the minds of others," Kirk said. "What happens to them when you've used their minds to increase your power?"

"Why do you care?" she countered. "With that wand you hold in your hand, you could reach out and shatter the stars if you knew how to use it." Her voice softened. "I offered once to share power with you. I offer again."

"No," Kirk said. "I don't know what you are. All I know is that you are not a woman. You are a destroyer."

"That's enough," she said. A phaser appeared in her hand. She aimed it at Kirk. "Give me the wand."

She extended her free hand, palm upward. "The wand—give it to me."

Kirk shrugged in surrender and held out the wand. She reached for it—and he dashed it to the stone floor. Sylvia screamed. Its crystal shattered. A blinding red light lit the corridor with the crimson of blood. It changed into the yellow dazzle of the sun. Then it was white like the light of a dead moon. When it faded, Kirk was standing on a rocky knoll. All around him was the bleak and barren surface of Pyris VII just as he'd first seen it. Only the fog was missing.

Dazed, McCoy said, "What happened, Jim?"

"That will take some explaining, Bones," Kirk told him.

Scott, recovered, said to Sulu, "Everything's vanished."

"Not quite everything," volunteered Spock.

On a rock ledge before them lay two tiny creatures, boneless, mere blobs of jelly, their bodies veined like those of jellyfish. One moved feebly. The other wavered up into the air, squeaking in a thin wail.

"Meet Korob and Sylvia in their true shape," Kirk said. "Their human shapes, like the castle and everything else, were illusion. Only the wand's crystal ball gave them an appearance of reality."

Spock's impassive face had a rare look of fascinated curiosity.

"A life form totally alien to our galaxy. If only we could study and preserve them."

The squeaking little creature was waving its transparent filaments over the now unmoving body of its companion. Soon, collapsing in on itself, it sank down beside it, its pitiful wail growing fainter.

"It's too late," McCoy said. "They're gone."

He sighed. "Illusion and reality. Sometimes I wonder if we humans will ever learn the difference."

WHERE NO MAN HAS GONE BEFORE

(Samuel A. Peeples)

Star date 1312.5 was a memorable one for the U.S.S. *Enterprise*. It marked the day of its first venture beyond the frontier of Earth's galaxy. The screen in its Briefing Room was already showing a strange vista—thinning stars etched against a coming night of depthless darkness broken only by the milky spots of phosphorescence which defined the existence of further galaxies millions of light years distant.

Kirk and Spock, a chessboard between them, looked away from the board to fix their eyes on the screen's center. It held, invisibly, an object detected by the *Enterprise* sensors; an object that was impossibly emitting the call letters of a starship known to be missing for two centuries.

Spock said, "Your move, Captain."

"We should be intercepting that thing now," Kirk said, frowning. "The bridge said they'd call . . ."

". . . any minute now." Spock finished the sentence for him. "I'll have you checkmated in your next move, sir."

"Have I ever mentioned that you play irritating chess, Mr. Spock?"

"Irritating? Ah yes, one of your Earth's emotions, I believe."

But Kirk had seen an opening for his bishop. Pouncing on the piece, he moved it. Spock's eyebrows went up.

"Certain that you don't know what irritation is?" Kirk asked.

Spock glowered at the board. "The fact that one of my ancestors was a human female is one, sir, I cannot . . ."

"Terrible, having bad blood like that," Kirk said sympathetically. "In addition to being checkmated, it could be called intolerable."

But the voice of Lieutenant Lee Kelso was speaking from the intercom. "Bridge to Briefing Room. Object now within tractor beam range, Captain."

"No visual contact yet, Lieutenant?"

"No, sir. Can't be a vessel. Reads only about one meter in diameter. Small enough to bring it aboard—if you want to risk it."

Kirk decided to risk it. It was a curious encounter on the edge of illimitable space. Curious—and just possibly informative. "The Transporter Room. Let's go, Mr. Spock," he said.

Scott was waiting for them at the console. "Materializer ready, sir, when you are."

"Bring it aboard," Kirk said.

The familiar hum came. And, with it, the platform's familiar shimmer, finally solidifying into the spherical shape of an old-style starship's recorder. Squatting on tripod legs, it stood about three feet in height, its metal surface seared, pockmarked. But it still identified itself by letters that read "U.S.S. *Valiant*"; and in smaller ones beneath them, "Galactic Survey Cruiser."

Kirk said, "That old-time variety of recorder could be ejected when something threatened its ship."

"In this case more probably destroyed its ship, sir," Spock said. "Look how it's burnt and pitted."

Kirk was approaching the platform when Scott said sharply, "Take care, sir! That thing's radioactive!"

Kirk stopped. "The Q signal, Mr. Scott."

Scott hit a button on his console. It beeped shrilly. As a pulsating glow enveloped the recorder, its antennae moved out and clicked into position.

"It's transmitting," Scott said.

"Interesting," said Spock. "I have a recorder monitoring . . ."

He was interrupted by Kelso's voice from the intercom. "All decks, six minutes to galaxy edge."

The galaxy's edge—where, as far as anyone knew, no man had ever gone before. Of course, there was no neat boundary to the edge of the galaxy; it just gradually thinned out. But in six minutes, the last of its stars and systems would be behind them.

"Yellow alert," Kirk said.

"Captain's orders—yellow alert, all decks," Kelso relayed it.

A moment later, an elevator slid open to emit Lieutenant Commander Gary Mitchell, now senior helmsman since Sulu had become ship's physicist. The promotion had won widespread approval—unnecessary, of course, but helpful; Mitchell was a popular officer. But during a yellow alert his normal chore was monitoring the artificial gravity system as well as the helm.

"Everything's in order, Jim," he said with a grin, as if reading Kirk's mind. "Kelso's voice sounded so nervous, I figured you'd left the bridge. Finish the game, Spock?"

"The Captain plays most illogically," the Science Officer complained. "I expected him to move his castle."

Kirk laughed, making a throat-cutting gesture for Mitchell's benefit. It was clear that the two were old, warm friends. In the bridge all three hurried to their positions. "Relieving you, Mr. Alden," Mitchell told the junior helmsman.

"Screen on," Kirk said. "Lieutenant Kelso, how far now to the galaxy edge?"

"Four minutes to our jumping-off point, sir."

"Alert off, Lieutenant Kelso." He turned to Mitchell. "Neutralize warp, Commander. Hold this position."

As the heavy throb of the ship's powerful engines eased, the bridge elevator opened. First to step out of it was Dr. Elizabeth Dehner, tall, slim, in her mid-twenties, a potentially beautiful woman if she had cared to be one, which she didn't. Other professional personnel followed her—senior physician, Dr. Piper, physicist Sulu, Engineering Chief Scott. Turning to Mitchell, Kirk said, "Address intercraft."

"Intercraft open, sir."

Kirk seized his speaker. "This is the Captain speaking. The object we encountered is a ship's disaster recorder, apparently ejected from the U.S.S. *Valiant* almost two hundred years ago. Mr. Spock is now explor-

ing its memory banks. We hope to learn how the
Valiant got this far, whether it probed out of the galaxy
and what destroyed the vessel. As soon as we have
those answers, we'll begin our own probe. All decks
stand by." He paused a moment. "All department
heads, check in, as per rota."

"Astro Sciences standing by, Captain," Sulu said.

"Engineering divisions ready as always," Scott's
voice said cheerfully. Nothing, not even the awesome
void now before them, could check his Gaelic self-
assurance for long.

"Life Sciences ready, sir," Dr. Piper's voice reported.
He was temporary—McCoy was on a special study
leave—and rather an elderly man for Starfleet service,
but he seemed to be a competent enough physician.
"Request permission to bring to the bridge my special
assistant, Dr. Dehner."

Elizabeth Dehner had joined the expedition at the
Aldebaran colony; Kirk had not yet had much chance
to talk to her, and now was not the time. But she might
be interested in the abyss now opening before them all.
"Granted."

The two appeared within a minute. Kirk said, "Dr.
Dehner, you're a psychiatrist, I'm told, assigned to
study crew reactions under extreme conditions."

"Quite correct, Captain."

Kirk gestured at the screen. "There's an extreme
condition. Millions upon millions of light years of abso-
lutely nothing, except a few molecules of ionized gas."

Spock called from his station. "Getting something
from the recorder now, Captain."

But Dr. Elizabeth Dehner had more to say. "Sir, I
shall be interested, too, in how the *Valiant*'s crew react-
ed to disaster."

Kirk eyed her curiously. Mitchell also appraised her,
a little smile on his handsome face. "You want to
improve the breed, Doctor?"

"I've heard that's more your own specialty, Commander," she said icily.

"Sock!" Mitchell murmured to Kelso. "It's a walking
refrigerator, by gum!" She overheard him. A flush crept
up and over her composed features.

Coded electronic beeps were sounding from the listening device Spock had applied to the recorder. He looked up as Kirk joined him. "Decoding memory banks," he said. "Captain's log now—reports the *Valiant* encountered a magnetic space storm that swept it back into this direction."

Kirk nodded. "The old impulse engines weren't strong enough to resist a thing like that."

Spock was leaning closer to his listener. "The storm flung it past this point . . . about a half light year out of the galaxy . . . they were thrown clear of the storm . . . then they seem to have headed back into the galaxy." He made a control adjustment. "I'm not getting it all. It sounds as though the ship were struggling with some unknown force."

The beeps grew louder. Interpreting, Spock said, "Confusion now . . . orders and counterorders . . . emergency power drains . . . repeated urgent requests for information from the ship's computer records." He stopped to look up at Kirk again. "They want to know everything there is to know about ESP in human beings!" He shook his head. "Odd, that. Very odd indeed."

"Extrasensory perception!" Kirk was incredulous. But he motioned to Elizabeth Dehner. "Dr. Dehner, what do you know about ESP?"

She went to the computer station. "In tests I've taken, my ESP rated rather high."

Kirk said, "I asked what you *know* about ESP."

She spoke with the pomp of the pedant. "It is a fact some people can sense future events, read the backs of playing cards and so on. But the Esper ability is always quite limited . . ."

Spock broke in. "Severe damage—no, make that severe injuries." His face was strained with listening concentration. "Seven crewmen dead . . . no, make that *six*—one crewman recovered." He looked up at Kirk once more. "It's the casualties that appear to have stimulated the interest in extrasensory perception. Interest is the wrong word. It seems to be driving them frantic."

Bent to the listener again, he suddenly stiffened. "No, this must be garbled. I'm getting something about 'Destruct.'" Frowning, he removed the earphone. "I must have read it incorrectly. It sounded as though the Captain had ordered the destruction of his own ship!"

Kirk turned questioningly to the department heads.

"You heard," he said. "Comments?"

Piper shrugged. "The only fact we have for sure is that the *Valiant* was destroyed."

"The fact," Kirk said, "which is the best argument to continue *our* probe. Other vessels will be heading out here some day—and they'll have to know what they'll be facing."

He strode back to his command chair. "Commander Mitchell, ahead, warp-factor one," he said. "We are leaving the galaxy."

As the *Enterprise* moved past the last stars, the bridge alarm light flashed. All eyes turned to the large viewing screen. Against the blackness of deep space a wispy pattern of colors was building up ahead of the ship.

Spock said, "Force field of some kind."

Mitchell said, "Whatever it is, we're coming up on it fast."

Kirk said nothing. Though distance from the phenomenon made certain judgment dangerous, it seemed to be some variety of impalpable barrier. Its colors were growing brighter, extending, interweaving into what appeared to a flaring, multicolored, massive curtain of pure energy. It might have been a monstrous space version of Earth's Aurora Borealis. And it was sending the bridge alarm siren into shrieks of warning.

He stared at it, hard-jawed. Its colors, radiating from the screen, rippled across the strained faces around him.

The auroral colors were blazing now. Suddenly, with a muted crackle, a circuit shorted.

"Field intensity rising . . ." Spock began.

As he spoke, the bridge lights died. For several seconds Kirk didn't notice their loss, the radiance from the screen had simultaneously become so brilliant that hands were rising instinctively to shield dazzled eyes.

Then a blinding whip of pure white light shot from the screen. At the same moment, an entire instrument panel went out in a shower of sparks and smoke. Another promptly shorted, with an angry crackle. The whole bridge seemed to be hazed in flying sparks. Elizabeth Dehner screamed and fell to the deck, writhing as if in the grip of some uncontrollable energy. Once down, she kept on screaming. The dial needles on Kirk's command board whirled.

"Helmsman!"

But the sparks had invaded Mitchell, too. Jerking like a marionette pulled by a madman's strings, he staggered to his feet and then went rigid. With a last galvanic convulsion, he toppled to the deck, inert, unconscious. His body rolled as the ship shuddered.

The confusion mounted, shock after shock, now joined by the mindless hysteria of the alarm siren. Kirk and Spock clung to their chairs; most of the others had been jolted out of theirs.

In the end, discipline triumphed while technology failed all around them. Painfully, inch by inch, Kirk dragged himself back to his command control panel. Kelso crawled over to his. Spock, stepping over the crumpled Mitchell, took over his helmsman's station. But the battering continued. Wrenched metal screeched as the *Enterprise* fought to hold itself together.

"Lateral power!" Kirk shouted. *"Crash speed. Take her out of this!"*

Spock and Kelso wrestled with controls. Power returned to the shaking ship. The bridge lights glimmered back on. The alarm siren quieted. But many of the instrument panels were dead with their circuits. Smoke from one still drifted through the bridge.

Kirk got to his feet. "Take damage reports, Mr. Spock."

Spock relayed the order to the ship's crew—and Piper lifted Elizabeth's head. Clinging to his arm, she climbed shakily to her feet. "Something hit me like an electrical charge," she whispered. Piper left her to go to Mitchell.

"Well?" Kirk asked.

"He's alive. Appears to be in shock."

Spock made his damage report. "Our main engines are out, Captain. We're on emergency power cells. Casualties—seven dead."

A moment prolonged itself. Then Kirk said, "Perhaps we are fortunate."

"Commander Mitchell is moving, sir," Spock said.

Kirk dropped to a knee beside his senior helmsman. "Gary! How do you feel?"

Mitchell's arm covered his eyes as though the screen's radiance still dazzled them. "Jim? Weak as a kitten—but better now. I think I'll live."

He moved the arm from his eyes. Their blue had turned into a gleaming metallic silver.

No amount of technical resourcefulness could repair the damage suffered by the crippled *Enterprise*. Moving now on impulse power alone, its dim bridge lights gave everybody the measure of the havoc. Kirk, considering his burned-out engines, remembered the burned recorder ejected by the *Valiant*. Had it survived the onslaught by that merciless radiation? If it had, what happened afterwards?

On his computer station screen, Spock was busily flashing the names of certain members of the ship's personnel. Among them were those of Elizabeth Dehner and Gary Mitchell. Noting them, Kirk gave Spock a sober look. Spock hastily flashed off Elizabeth's name as she approached them.

"Autopsy report, Captain," she said. "Each case showed damage to the body's neural circuits—an area of the brain burned out."

"And you?" Kirk said. "Feeling all right now?"

"Much better. And Commander Mitchell is, too, except for the eyes. We're trying to find a reason for those. And why, of all the people in the crew, only certain ones were affected."

Spock spoke quietly. "I think we have found that answer."

"You said that tests show you have a high degree of extrasensory perception, Doctor," Kirk reminded her.

"The others who were affected have it, too. Gary Mitchell has the highest ESP rating of all."

She was clearly puzzled. "I suppose it's conceivable the Esper ability attracted some force." Then she shrugged. "But if you're suggesting there's something dangerous in that . . ."

Spock interrupted. "Before the *Valiant* was destroyed, its Captain was frantically searching for ESP information on his crew members."

"Espers are merely people who have flashes of—well, *insight*," she said.

"Aren't there also those who seem able to see through solid objects?" Spock asked. "Or can cause fires to start spontaneously?"

The question irritated her. "ESP is nothing more than a sort of sixth sense. There's nothing about it that can make a person dangerous!"

"I take it you're speaking of *normal* ESP power, Doctor," Spock said.

"Perhaps you know of another kind!" she flared.

Kirk intervened. "Do you know for sure, Doctor, that there *isn't* another kind?"

An angry disdain sharpened her voice. "I have work to do," she said. "You must excuse me." She left them to move quickly to the elevator.

In Sickbay, Mitchell, propped up against pillows, was sufficiently recovered to use his reading viewer. The eyes that followed its turning pages were as gleamingly silver as quicksilver. Kirk, entering, watched him read for a long moment. Without looking up, Mitchell snapped off the reading viewer to say, "Hello, Jim."

He hadn't even been obliged to turn his head to identify his caller. For some reason this realization troubled Kirk. He sat down in the chair beside the bed. "Hey, you look worried," Mitchell said.

Kirk forced a smile. "I've been worried about you since that girl on Deneb IV."

Mitchell nodded reminiscently. "She was a nova, that one," he said. "But there's nothing to worry about. Except for the eyes, I'm fine." He grinned his charming grin. "They kind of stare back at me when I'm shaving."

"Vision all right?"

"Twenty-twenty."

"Nothing else, Gary?"

Mitchell looked up curiously at Kirk's tone. "Like what, for instance?"

"Do you—feel any different in yourself?"

"In a way, I feel better than I ever felt before in my life." He paused. "It actually seems to have done me some good."

"Oh. How?"

Mitchell gestured toward the reading viewer. "I'm getting a chance to bone up on some of that long-hair stuff you like. Man, I remember you at the Academy! A stack of books with legs! The first thing I heard from upper classmen was 'Watch out for Lieutenant Kirk! In his class you either *think*—or you sink.' "

"Oh, come on," Kirk said. "I wasn't that bad."

"You weren't *what?*" Mitchell laughed. "Do you remember almost washing me out?"

"I sort of leaned on cadets I liked," Kirk said.

"Man, if I hadn't aimed that little blond lab technician at you . . ."

"You *what?*" Kirk stared at him. "You mean you actually *planned* that?"

"You wanted me to *think*, didn't you? So I *thought*. I outlined her whole campaign for her."

Kirk found it hard to return the grin. "Gary, I almost married her!"

"I sort of lean, too, on people I like. She said you came through great."

Kirk, remembering, struggled with his dismay. He repeated, "Gary, I almost *married* her."

"Better be good to me," Mitchell said. He pointed again to the reading viewer. "I'm getting even better ideas from *that*."

Kirk looked at the tape on the viewer. "Spinoza?"

"That's one," Mitchell said. "Once you get into him, he's simple. Childish, almost. By the way, I don't agree with him at all."

"No?" Kirk said. "Go on."

"Go on where? So I'm finally doing some reading."
The cold, silver glitter of his eyes made an uncomfortable contrast with the easy warmth of his manner.
His white teeth flashed again in the charming grin. "I'm saying I'm fine! When do I go back on duty?"

Kirk hesitated. "I want Dr. Dehner to keep you under observation for a while yet."

Mitchell groaned. "With almost a hundred women on board, you choose *that* one to hang around me!"

"Think of it as a challenge," Kirk said.

The silver eyes fixed on him. "That's not so friendly, James, my friend. Didn't I say you'd better be good to me?"

The mutually gauging moment passed. Finally Mitchell shook his head in mock resignation. Then he pointedly turned back to the reading viewer. Kirk, more troubled than before, didn't speak, either, as he got to his feet and left Sickbay.

Behind him, Mitchell increased the speed of the viewer's turning pages. He read fast—a man locking facts into his mind with an incredible rapidity.

An image of the turning pages was showing on Spock's library computer screen. When Kirk joined him, they were turning so quickly that their movement was blurred. Spock said, "He's reading faster with every passing second. Is that Gary Mitchell? The slowpoke reader we used to know?"

Kirk took three paces away from the screen and returned. "Put a twenty-four hour watch on Sickbay. The fullest possible range of examinations and tests."

The results gave joy to the heart of Piper. "Perfect—perfect," he murmured as he completed his final checkup. "Such perfect health is rare." He tapped the body function panel as though it were hard to credit the veracity of its readings.

"Great in all departments, right?" said Mitchell. Bored, he spoke to Elizabeth. "Too bad psychiatry isn't an exact science, eh, Doctor? Be nice to have a dial that showed the level of a patient's sanity."

"I am aware that you don't particularly like me, Commander," she said. "But since I'm assigned here, can we make the best of it?"

"I've got nothing against you, Doctor."

"Or against the 'walking refrigerator'?"

He was openly startled. "Sorry about that." All his charm went into the three words.

"Women professionals do tend to overcompensate," she said. "Now let's talk about you. How do you feel? Tell me everything."

"Everything about what? Everyone seems worried because I don't have a fever or something." He pointed to the body function panel. "Now old Piper's gone, maybe I can make you happy by changing those readings . . ."

The panel's normal levels altered into abnormal ones. Elizabeth stared at them and back at Mitchell. Slightly shaken himself, he said, "Now the normal readings again . . ."

The levels dropped back to normal.

"How did you do that?" Elizabeth demanded.

"I'm not sure. I—just thought of making it happen. Then it happened." He eyed the panel. "It's not the instruments. It's me. Something I do inside. Hey, watch this . . ."

All the panel's levels plummeted to zero.

Elizabeth grabbed his hand. "Stop it!" she cried. "Stop it now!"

The gauge needles quivered. Rising swiftly up from the "death" indication, they came to rest at normal.

Mitchell stared at them, too. He had paled; and Elizabeth, appalled, said, "For twenty-two seconds you were *dead!* No life function at all!"

Mitchell suddenly realized she was holding his hand. Reddening, she tried to pull hers away but he held it fast. "Hang on a minute, baby. I'm scared. There've been other things, too. Like going halfway through the ship's library in hardly a day. What's happened to me?"

"Do you remember everything you read that quickly?"

He nodded. She took a tape from his bedside table. "On any tape? How about this one? Do you remember page 387?"

"Sure," he said. "It's *The Nightingale Woman* written by Tarbolde on a Canopus planet back in 1996. It begins, 'My love has wings, Slender, feathered things, With grace in upswept curve and tapered tip—' " He stopped, amused. "Funny you should pick that one."

"Why?"

"It's one of the most passionate love poems of the last couple of centuries."

She pulled her hand from his. He watched her do it, smiling. "How do *you* feel?" he asked.

"What? Oh, you mean that electrical blast! It just knocked me down. That's all."

"You're very sure?"

She wasn't sure of anything in the presence of this man with the silver eyes so bright upon her. But somehow, she suspected that she'd given herself away. She was glad when the knock came at the door. It was Kelso. "I was on my coffee break," he told them, "and thought I'd just check up on Gary here."

"It's OK, Lee," Mitchell said. "Come on in."

It was Kelso's first full view of the changed eyes. They disconcerted him. Mitchell laughed. "Don't let my gorgeous orbs throw you, chum. The lady doctor here likes them, don't you, beautiful Doctor?"

Surprised, Kelso said, "Oh. Yeah. Sure."

"How goes the repair work?"

"The main engines are gone." Kelso's face grew somber. "And they'll stay gone, too, unless we can find some way of re-energizing them."

Mitchell frowned. "You'd better check on the starboard impulse packs. The points have decayed to lead." At Kelso's look of amazement, he said, "I'm not joking, pal. So wipe the shock off your face. You activate those packs—and you'll blow up the whole impulse deck!"

The hardness in his voice got through to Kelso. "Sure," he said hastily. "I'll get on to them right away. I—I just wanted to say I'm glad you're all right."

Mitchell glared angrily after him. "The fool! He's seen those rotten points a hundred times but is too dumb to notice their condition!"

"How did *you* know about them?" Elizabeth asked.

The arrogance was suddenly gone. "I don't know. Maybe the image of what he saw was still in his mind and I—I could see it in his mind." The silver eyes were looking up at her out of a bewildered, very frightened face.

In the Briefing Room, Kelso was pointing to the fused tip in a starboard impulse pack. "It made no sense at all that he'd know about this," he said to Kirk. "But naturally I took a look at the packs anyway. And he's right! This point's burned out just as he described it!"

Each in turn, the Science Department heads examined the piece of metal on the Briefing Room table. Elizabeth opened the door. "Sorry I'm late, Captain. I became so interested in observing Gary—Commander Mitchell—that I . . ."

Spock said, "The subject under discussion is not Commander Mitchell, Doctor. We are concerned with what he is mutating into."

Her face tightened with anger. "I know Vulcans lack human feeling, but to talk like that about a man you've worked next to for years . . ."

"That's enough, Doctor!" Kirk said.

"No, it isn't!" she cried. "I understand you least of all! Gary's told me you've been friends ever since he joined the service! You even asked him to join your first command!"

Kirk kept his voice level. "It is my duty, Doctor, to note the reports, observations, even speculations on any subject which affects the safety of this ship." He nodded toward Spock. "And it is my Science Officer's duty to see that I'm provided with them. Go ahead, Mr. Spock."

Spock addressed Elizabeth. "Has he shown any evidence of unusual powers to you?"

She didn't mention the tricks he'd played with the body function panel. Instead, she chose to say, "He can control certain autonomic reflexes. He reads very fast; and retains more than most of us consider usual."

Kirk spoke sharply. "Repeat what you just told us, Mr. Scott."

"About an hour ago," Scott said, "the bridge controls started going crazy. Levers shifted all by themselves. Buttons were pressed without fingers to press them. Instrument readings wavered from safety points to danger ones."

"And on my monitor screen," Spock said, "I saw the Commander smile each time it happened. He treated the confusion he caused as though this ship and its crew were toys created for his amusement."

"Is that correct, Dr. Dehner?" Kirk queried. "Does he show abilities of that magnitude?"

"I've seen some such indications," she said.

Piper spoke up. "And you didn't think that worth the concern of the Captain?"

"No one's been hurt!" she protested. "Don't any of you understand? A mutated superior man could be a wonderful asset to the race—the forerunner of a new and better kind of human being!"

Kirk, looking at her exalted face, thought, Idealism gone rampant again! My God! He turned with relief to Sulu.

"If you want the mathematics on this, sir," Sulu said, "the Commander's ability is increasing geometrically. It's like owning a penny that doubles every day. In a month you'd be a millionaire."

Spock said, "In less time than that, Mitchell will attain powers we can neither understand nor cope with. What happens when we're not only useless to him—but actual annoyances?"

Elizabeth, about to speak, decided for silence. Kirk glanced around the table. "There'll be no discussion of this with the crew. Thank you. That's all."

The room emptied of everyone but Spock. Kirk turned to see his Science Officer inspecting him, creases of worry in his forehead. He spoke with careful deliberateness. "We will never reach an Earth base with Mitchell aboard, sir. You heard the mathematics of it. In a month he'll have as much in common with us as we'd have with a ship full of white mice."

His own anxiety oppressing him, Kirk snapped, "I need recommendations, Mr. Spock—not vague warnings."

"Recommendation number one. The planet, Delta-Vega, is only a few light days away from here. It has a lithium-cracking station. If we could adapt some of its power packs to our engines . . ."

"And if we can't, we'll be trapped in orbit there. We haven't the power to blast back out of it."

"It's the only possible way to get Mitchell off this ship, sir."

"If you mean strand him there, I won't do it. The station is fully automated. There's not a soul on the whole planet. Even ore ships call there only once every twenty years."

"Then you have only one other choice," Spock said. "Kill Mitchell while you can."

"Get out of here!" Kirk yelled.

Imperturbable, Spock repeated, "That's your only other choice. Assuming you take it while you still have time."

Kirk slammed his fist on the table. "Will you try for one moment to *feel?* We're talking about Gary Mitchell!"

"The Captain of the *Valiant* probably felt as you do, sir. But he waited too long to make his decision. I think we have both guessed that."

Kirk groped for a chair. Spock turned one around for him. He sank down in it, his face in his hands. After a moment, he removed them. Nodding to Spock, he said, "Set course for Delta-Vega."

Mitchell's powers were indeed expanding. And he'd begun to exult in exerting them. Lying in his Sickbay bed, he suddenly decided to snap his fingers. The lights flicked off. He waved a hand—and the lights blazed back. He sat up on the bed's edge, eyeing other portions of his room. He pointed a finger at a table. It soared into the air, teetered insanely on one leg and dropped quietly back into place.

"I am thirsty!" he abruptly announced to nobody.

Across the room, a metal cup on the water dispenser slid under the spigot. Water flowed from it. The filled cup lifted, and floating through the air, settled into

Mitchell's outstretched hand. He was sipping from it when Kirk, with Spock and Elizabeth, came in.

"I feel great," Mitchell told them. "So don't bother to inquire into my state of health. Sometimes I think there's nothing I can't do. And some people believe that makes a monster of me, don't they?"

"Are you reading all our thoughts, Gary?" Kirk asked.

"Just in flashes so far—mostly strong thoughts like fear. For instance, you, Jim. You're worried about the safety of this ship."

"What would you do in my place?"

"Just what Mr. Spock is thinking—kill me while you can." Lifting his hand, he pointed a finger at Kirk. A bolt of radiance shot from it—and stunned, Kirk toppled over. Spock leaped at Mitchell—but before he could touch him, he, too, had crashed to the floor.

Elizabeth seized Mitchell's arm. "Stop it, Gary!"

He looked down at Kirk who was struggling back to his feet. "Sure, I know a lot," he said. "I know you're orbiting Delta-Vega, Jim. I can't let you maroon me there. I may not want to leave the ship, not yet. I may want another place. I'm not sure what kind of world I can use."

"*Use?*" Elizabeth said, shocked by the word's implications.

"Yes, beautiful Doctor. I don't get it all yet, but if I keep on growing, I'll be able to do things a god can do."

Spock sprang up. He struck Mitchell with a force that knocked him from the bed. He started to rise and Kirk landed a hard, fast blow on his jaw. His legs gave way. Groggy, he sprawled, supporting himself by his hands and knees. Breathing heavily, Kirk whirled to Elizabeth. "I want him unconscious for a while."

She took a hypogun from her medical case. Gas hissed as she touched Mitchell's shoulder with it. He subsided, spread-eagled, at their feet.

But another shot was required. This time Piper administered it in the Transporter Room where its technicians were preparing the beam-down to the surface of Delta-Vega. But the torpor induced by the second shot lasted for less time than the unconsciousness caused by the first one. Mitchell came out of it to begin to struggle so fiercely that he pulled himself free of the combined hold of Kirk and Spock. "Fools!" he said thickly. "Soon I will squash you all like crawling insects!"

Piper moved quickly in for a third shot. Mitchell slumped again. Dragging at him, Kirk and Spock rushed him over to the Transporter platform. The other members of the landing party hastened to their positions on it. Mitchell was swaying back onto his feet when Kirk shouted, *"Energize!"*

They materialized before the lithium-cracking plant.

From what could be seen of Delta-Vega's surface, it was a genuinely alien planet. Its soil was dust of a muddy blue color, and the vegetation that sprouted from it was brassy, scaled and knobbed like crocodile skin. Black boulders, their fissures filled with the blue dust, abounded—the only familiar aspect of the landscape. In the distance, a mountain of the black rock shouldered up against the horizon. But Kirk's concerns were other than the weird phenomena of the uninhabited planet. The hypos had finally got to Mitchell. Spock and Communications Officer Alden were supporting him into the building's entrance.

"Can we make it, Lee?" Kirk asked Kelso.

"If we can bypass the fuel bins without blowing ourselves up, we can make it, Captain." Kelso was gazing up at the installation. It was enormous, stretching its huge towers, metallic vats, its strangely coiling ells of complex instrumentation in all directions. Elizabeth stooped to touch a scaly flowerlike growth. It was burning hot.

"And not a soul on this planet but us?" she said.

Kirk answered her briefly. "Just us, Doctor. Lee, let's find the control room of this place."

They couldn't miss it. Doorless, it faced them in the building's central hall. Except for its contour, its size, the steady drone of its automated mechanisms, it bore some resemblance to the *Enterprise* bridge. Its walls were ranked by the same type of instrument panels, the same arrangements of meters, switches and dials. Kelso and Communications Officer Alden went at once to work selecting panels for later beam-up to the *Enterprise* Engineering section. A detail of other crewmen busied themselves with the thick electronic cables that would be needed to interlink the panels left to maintain the cracking plant's operation.

Kirk watched thoughtfully. "Those fuel bins, Lee. They could be detonated from here. A destruct switch?"

Kelso looked up, surprised. "I guess a destruct switch could be wired into this panel, sir."

"Do it," Kirk said.

Kelso stared at him. Then he nodded—and Spock spoke from the doorless entrance. "Mitchell's regained full consciousness, Captain. Perhaps you'd better come."

He had been confined in a maximum security room, one made escape-proof not by bars and bolts but by the invisible fence of a force field. He was pacing the room like a caged tiger. Outside, Piper, Elizabeth beside him, held his hypogun at the ready. Near them, an *Enterprise* security guard, phaser in hand, kept his eyes on the furious tiger.

"I want only one medical officer here at any one time," Kirk said. "The other will monitor him on the dispensary screen."

"I'd like my turn now," Elizabeth said. "I want to try and talk to him "

Piper nodded, handing her the hypogun. As he left, Kirk, pressing a button, tested the force field. It crackled sharply. Mitchell stopped pacing. Eyeing Kirk across the barrier, he said, "My friend, James Kirk. Remember the rodent things on Dimorus, the poisoned darts they threw? I took one meant for you . . ."

"And almost died. I remember," Kirk said.

"Then why be afraid of me now, Jim?"

"Gary, you have called us insects to be squashed if we got in your way."

"I was drugged then!"

"And before that, you said you'd kill a mutant like yourself were you in my place."

"Kill me then! Spock is right! And you're a fool not to do it!"

Elizabeth cried, "Gary, you don't mean that!"

He spoke directly to her. "In time, beautiful Doctor,

you will understand, in time. Humans cannot survive if a race of true Espers like me is born. That's what Spock knows—and what that fool there," he nodded toward Kirk, "is too sentimental to know." He moved toward the force field sealing off his security room. As he neared it, there was a screech of high voltage. A spray of sparks flew up, scattered and died.

Spock and the guard had drawn their phasers. But Mitchell continued to push against the force field. For a moment his whole body glowed red. But through the brightness Kirk saw that the old human blueness of his eyes had replaced the silver. Then the force field flung him away. He staggered backward and fell on the room's bunk. He sank down on it, his face in his hands, groaning.

Kirk said, "His eyes returned to normal."

"Fighting the force field drained his strength." Spock studied the swaying figure on the bunk. "He could be handled now, Captain."

"Handled," Mitchell said. He looked up. His eyes were shining with so bright a silver that the room seemed lit with silver. "I grow stronger with every passing second. I thought you knew that, Spock."

Kirk snapped his communicator open. "Put full energy on this force field, Lieutenant Kelso."

There was a louder hum as power poured into the force field. A visible radiance began to gather around it.

Mitchell rose from the bunk. He rose from it to smile at Kirk from the other side of his barricade.

But if he remained Kirk's rankling thorn of anxiety, there was good news from the *Enterprise*. In its Engine Room a charred control panel had been successfully replaced by one beamed up from the cracking station. More new panels were required. So Kelso was still busy with the heavy cables he was using for the connecting link among the station's remaining panels.

Over his communicator, Scott said, "It fits like a glove, Captain. Did Mr. Spock get that phaser rifle we beamed down?"

At Kirk's surprised look, Spock moved the heavy weapon from the wall he'd laid it against. Kirk shook his head in a wordless sadness before he answered Scott. "Affirmative, Scotty. Landing party out."

"Mitchell tried to break through the force field again," Spock said tonelessly. "And his eyes changed faster. Nor did he show any signs of weakness this time."

"Dr. Dehner feels he isn't that dangerous," Kirk said. "What makes you right and a trained psychiatrist wrong?"

"Because she *feels*," Spock said. "Her feelings for Mitchell weaken the accuracy of her judgment. Mine tell me we'll be lucky if we can repair the ship and get away from him before he becomes very dangerous indeed."

"Captain!" Kelso called. Wearily Kirk crossed over to him. He looked at the sheathed switch Kelso had attached to a panel. It had been painted red. "Direct to the power bins," Kelso said. "From here a man could blow up the whole valley, Captain."

"Lee," Kirk said. "Lee, if Mitchell gets out—at your discretion, positioned here, you'll be the last chance. Lee, if he gets out—I want you to hit that switch."

The full meaning of Kirk's words struck Kelso dumb. If he hit the red switch, he'd go where the valley went. He looked at the switch and back into Kirk's eyes. After a moment, he managed a very sober, "Yes, sir."

In other circumstances, regeneration of the *Enterprise* engines would have been cause for rejoicing. The ship was ready for takeoff. The working detail of crewmen had been transported back up to it. But Mitchell's condition had worsened.

Now his skin tones had altered. What had once been ruddy flesh had a silvery cast, suggesting solid metal. He stood, arms folded across his chest, looking at them across the force field. If he noticed Spock's phaser rifle, he gave no sign of it.

"He's been like this for hours," Elizabeth said.

A silver man. "Have Dr. Piper meet us in the control

room with Kelso," Kirk said. "We'll all beam up to the ship together."

"That's risky, sir," Spock said. "If we take our eyes off him . . ."

"Kelso will be on the destruct switch until the last minute." Kirk gestured to the silent figure behind the force field. "I think he knows that."

Elizabeth said, "I'm staying with him."

Kirk spoke flatly. "You'll leave with the ship, Doctor."

"I can't," she said. "I'm sorry."

Kirk's communicator beeped. "Kirk here," he said.

"The station seems to be running fine, sir," Kelso said. "Even without its quota of panels. The cables have done the job. Fission chamber three checks."

Behind him one of the cables stirred. It began to crawl toward him, snakelike. Slithering, silent, it lifted from the floor, twisting itself into loops. Abruptly, but still silently, a loop rose high into the air—and dropped over Kelso's head. A noose, flexible, inexorable, it tightened around his neck. Helplessly, Kelso tore at it, choking. Then he fell to the floor.

Mitchell smiled into Kirk's eyes. There was something ghastly in the movement of his silver lips. But Elizabeth saw only the smile.

"You see?" she cried to Kirk. *"He's not evil!"*

"You will leave with the ship, Doctor," Kirk repeated.

Mitchell spoke. "You should have killed me when you could, James. Compassion and command are an idiot's mixture."

Kirk grabbed Spock's phaser rifle. Mitchell's hand made a gesture that included them both. Flame blazed from it. As they collapsed, Mitchell walked to the force field. He brushed it as one brushes aside a flimsy curtain. A single spark flared briefly. He passed through the portal to stand face to face with Elizabeth. Taking her hand, he led her back into his room and over to a wall mirror. "Look at yourself, beautiful Doctor," he said.

She screamed. Then she flung her hands over her face to shut out the sight of her silver eyes.

Kirk wavered slowly back into consciousness. Pale, drained-looking, Piper was stooping over him. "Whatever it was, Captain, it affected me, too. Swallow this capsule." He paused. "Kelso's dead. Strangled. At least Spock is still alive."

"Dr. Dehner?" Kirk whispered.

"She's gone with Mitchell. That capsule will restore your strength in a minute or so. I must insert one in Spock's mouth. He's still unconscious and . . ."

"What direction did they take?" Kirk asked.

"Toward the rock mountain."

Kirk struggled to his knees. He reached for the phaser rifle he had dropped. As he checked it, he said, "As soon as Mr. Spock recovers, you will both immediately transport up to the *Enterprise*."

Piper looked up from his work of massaging the capsule down Spock's throat. "Captain, you're not—" he began.

"Where," Kirk continued inflexibly, "if you have not received a signal from me in twelve hours, you will proceed at maximum warp to the nearest Earth base. You will inform it that this entire planet is to be subjected to a lethal concentration of neutron radiation."

The capsule was working. He found he was able to stand. "No protest on this, Doctor Piper! It's an order!"

He slung the rifle over his shoulder and walked out of the cracking station.

The approach to the rock mountain's craggy escarpments made harsh going for Mitchell and Elizabeth. The sharp black stones and slithery blue sand which composed the terrain of Delta-Vega had not been created for pleasant afternoon strolls. As a sudden breeze blew sand into her face, Elizabeth panted, "It— it would take a miracle to survive here."

"Sit down," Mitchell said. "I'll make one."

He made a gesture. The blue sand around them darkened into the rich brown of loam. It shifted to give way to an upspring of bubbling water. The scaly, brass-colored vegetation turned green. From a patch of it, the leafy trunk of a peach tree rose up. Fruit hung from its boughs. Mitchell bent to drink from the spring.

When she had quenched her thirst, he said, "You'll share this power, too. As you develop, you'll feel like me, able to make a world into anything you want it to be. Soon we will fully control our bodies. We'll never grow old. You're woman enough now to like that. Always young, as beautiful as you desire to be . . ."

He suddenly stiffened.

"What's wrong?" she asked anxiously.

"A visitor," he said. "A very foolish visitor."

"Who is it?"

"You'll enjoy playing God, Elizabeth."

A splinter of unnameable fear jabbed her. He laughed at the look on her face. "Blasphemy scares you?" He flung his arms wide, the silver hands outspread. "Let there be food! Give me Kaferian apples, world, my world!"

A squat, odd-shaped tree appeared, heavy with huge red fruit. Mitchell, detaching an apple from it, bit into it, its rich yellow juice running down his silver chin. "Whenever we'd stop at that planet, I'd stock up on these," he said. "What is *your* wish? Just speak it."

Her answer came in the form of a slow, thoughtful question. "How much have I changed, Gary?"

But he wasn't listening. He had turned to concentrate his gaze on the still unseen figure of Kirk clambering over boulders, the heavy weight of the phaser rifle on his shoulder.

Mitchell spoke. "Can you hear me, James? You can't see me, I know. So let me comfort you. You're on the right path. You'll see me soon. Soon enough."

Kirk stopped. He had heard the words. How, he didn't know. He started to unlimber the rifle when he realized that Mitchell wasn't there. He resumed climbing.

"It's Captain Kirk," Elizabeth said as though speaking to herself. "In my mind I can see him."

"Go and meet him," Mitchell said. "Talk to him. Now that you're changing, you've got to discover how unimportant they are."

Hesitating, she stepped forward. Kirk sensed the presence on the shallow cliff above him, grabbed his rifle—and recognized the girl. Climbing up to her, he saw the hard silver of her eyes for the first time.

"Yes," she said. "It just took a little longer for it to happen to me."

Kirk lowered the rifle. "You've got to help me stop it, Dr. Dehner. Before it goes too far with you, too."

"I've already gone far enough to—to realize what he's doing is right. It's right for us."

"And for humans?" Kirk said. "You're still partly human—or you wouldn't be with him."

She looked away from him. Without certainty, she said, "Earth is—really unimportant. Before long, we'll be where it would take millions of years of learning for humans to reach."

"How will *he* learn if he skips over those millions of years?" Kirk said. "You don't know. You can't know. *He won't have lived through them!*"

"*Please*," she said. "Go back while you can!"

"You heard him joke about compassion. Above all a god needs compassion, Elizabeth."

"Go back!" she shouted.

"You were a psychiatrist," Kirk said. "You know the savage we all keep buried—the primitive self we dare not expose. But he'll dare to expose his! In God's name, Doctor, make your prognosis!"

Her face was tortured. Then she whispered, "He's coming!"

But he was already here. He ignored Kirk to speak to the girl. "I'm disappointed in you, Elizabeth. You still have doubts."

Whipping up his rifle, Kirk fired it at him. A fiery beam lanced out of it and struck him full in the chest. Its redness faded. Mitchell raised a finger. The rifle tore from Kirk's grasp to clatter on the stones beside him.

Time passed. Then Mitchell broke the silence. "I have been meditating," he said. "I have been reflecting upon the death of an old friend. His death and his honorable burial."

Kirk turned. Behind him, brown earth was scooping itself out into the neat shape of a grave. Elizabeth stared at Mitchell in unbelief. Trembling, she looked back at the grave. At its head stood a tidy, white military cross bearing the inscription "James R. Kirk. C-1277.1 to 1313.7."

A grinding sound came from overhead. Kirk looked up. A huge, rectangular rock slab was detaching itself from the cliff wall. It wobbled for a moment. Then it teetered into position directly above the grave.

Elizabeth screamed. "No, Gary, no!"

"You still like what you're seeing?" Kirk asked her.

"Time to pray, Captain," Mitchell said.

"To you?" Kirk said. "Not to both of you?"

The silver finger pointed at him. He was struck to his knees by the flash that darted from it. He remained on his knees, his eyes on the girl. "This is a jealous god, Elizabeth. In the end there will be one of you."

"Your last chance, Kirk!"

Elizabeth tensed. Sparks suddenly crackled between her and Mitchell. He reeled, recovered—and extended a silver hand toward her. A storm of sparks broke from it. She staggered, moaning with pain. But the energy drain had told on Mitchell. For a single second his eyes went blue. Then they were impervious silver once more. And once more the silver hand was extended toward the girl. A fiery mantle of sparks engulfed her. She crumpled. "Hurry," she whispered to Kirk. "There's—so little time."

The second outlay of energy had been expensive. Realizing his weakness, Mitchell turned to run. Kirk hurled himself forward and made a grab for his legs. A booted foot caught him in the chest. Then Mitchell seized a jagged rock. Kirk dodged the blow and closed with him.

"Gary, listen! For this moment you are human again . . ."

"It's gone now!" On a new surge of power, Mitchell smashed Kirk down with a silver fist.

He hit the ground hard, almost falling into the open grave. Then Mitchell was on him. In dizzy changes his face turned from silver to flesh. The silver won. Wrestling with him, Kirk could feel his whole body transforming itself into metal. He wrenched himself free, and had reached the rifle when Mitchell ripped an edged section of rock from the outcropping above them. It brushed his shoulder at the same moment he fired the rifle.

The beam missed Mitchell. But it struck the soft blue sand beneath the overhanging slab of rock that was to be his tombstone. It toppled and fell toward the grave.

"Gary!" Kirk shouted. "Look out!"

It was too late. Stumbling backward, Mitchell tripped. The rock slab hit him, tumbling him into the grave. A cloud of blue dust rose. When it settled, it had filled the letters etched into the broken white military cross.

Kirk kneed himself over to Elizabeth. The silver had gone from her eyes. "It's—all over, isn't it?" The voice was so weak that he had to stoop to hear it. Her head lolled over Kirk's arm. She was dead.

He got to his feet, a lonely stranger on a strange planet in a strange galaxy. But his communicator was familiar.

He spoke into it, his voice very tired. "Kirk to *Enterprise*. Come in, *Enterprise*."

It was almost as strange to be back in his command chair. He'd been a far way. The magnetic space storm— Delta-Vega—Mitchell's death—Kelso's—were they all events that had occurred in a dream? The new control panels around him were blinking as steadily as though they were the old ones. It was good to see Spock just standing there beside him.

"Ready to leave orbit, sir," Scott called from Kelso's old position.

"*Engage*," Kirk said. He switched on his Captain's log. "Add to official casualties, Dr. Elizabeth Dehner. Be it noted that she gave her life in performance of her duty. And Lieutenant Commander Gary Mitchell. The same notation."

He looked at Spock. "After all, he didn't ask for what happened to him. I want his service record to end that way."

Spock's Mephisto features were tranquil. "I felt for him, too, sir, strange to say."

Kirk eyed him speculatively. "Watch yourself, Mr. Spock," he said. "Your compassion is showing."

WOLF IN THE FOLD

(Robert Bloch)

The planet Argelius boasted the most popular Venusbergs in the galaxy. And spacemen's favorite was a café that featured the belly-dancing of the lushly exotic Kara. The other lovely women who companioned its male guests at their tables were an old, if still pleasing story to Kirk and McCoy. But they were a blissfully new one to Scott. He sat with them, glancing around him, enraptured. Then his eyes returned to Kara's sinuous grace as she twisted it on the dance floor, her transparent gold skirt swirling around her.

Beaming, Scott said unnecessarily, "I like Argelius."

"Very little about it not to like," Kirk said.

"You mean to tell me these women, these beauties— I mean, all this is . . ."

"The Argelians think very highly of pleasure," Kirk told him.

McCoy laughed. "There's an understatement if ever I heard one! This is a completely hedonistic society."

"Like Kara, Scotty?" Kirk asked.

There was a fervent "Aye!" from Scott, at which Kirk said, "Good. I've invited her to join us. It occurred to me you might like to meet her."

"Now that's what I call a Captain!" Scott exclaimed. "Always thinking of his men."

"You're not drinking, Jim," McCoy said. "The few polyesters in this native extract—good for the soul. Not to mention the body."

"I don't suppose a little loosener-upper would hurt." Kirk sipped his drink.

Scott, his eyes on Kara, said, "Mr. Spock should see us now."

McCoy snorted. "He'd just be 'fascinated' by the picturesque folk costumes in the place."

Kara had come to a spinning stop, her hands slanted over her eyes in the immemorially seductive gesture of simulated prudery. The café's dimness lit with sparks as though someone had released a swarm of fireflies. Scott pounded enthusiastically on the table.

Amused, Kirk said, "It's an Argelian custom to demonstrate one's approval by blinking delight lights."

"You telling an old Glasgow pub crawler how to applaud, Captain?" Scott said. Then all three men rose from their table. Kara was gliding toward them. As she approached, Kirk noted a young man at the bar. He had shoved his drink aside, his face darkened by a scowl. It deepened when Scott seated the girl beside him. Suddenly the scowler seized his drink, drained it and walked out of the café. Nor was the dancer's elderly musician pleased by the warmth of her smile at Scott. Laying aside his flutelike instrument, he averted his eyes from their table.

Scott, oblivious of everything but Kara's nearness, leaned forward to place his hand over hers.

"Tis a fine foggy night tonight," he said. "Did anyone ever tell you about the grand fogs we have in Edinburgh?"

"Never a word," she said. "But I'm dying to learn."

"Then why don't I show you? There's naught like a walk in a fog with a bonny lass."

"Or a handsome gentleman. Why don't we go?"

The sun on Scott's face would have dispersed even an Edinburgh fog. Kara's hand still in his, he got up. "You don't mind, do you?" he asked the others. "I might even get back to the ship on time."

"Don't hurry, Scotty," Kirk said. "Relax and enjoy yourself. That's what Argelius is all about."

He looked thoughtfully after them as they left. "My work is never done, Bones."

"*My* work, Jim. This is strictly prescription stuff. That explosion that threw Scotty against the bulkhead was caused by a woman."

"You're sure the physical damage is all cleared up?"

"Yes. But the psychological damage? I didn't like his resentment of all women after it happened."

"I defy any man to stay angry at women on a planet like this."

"When Scotty gets back to the ship, Jim, he may hate *you* for making him leave Argelius. But I'll bet my professional reputation he'll be finished with any lingering dislike of women."

"Well," Kirk said, "I think we've accomplished what we came here for. Bones, there's a spot across town where the women are so . . ."

"I know the place," McCoy interrupted. "Let's go."

The fog outside was thicker than they had expected. Light from the door they opened was diffused against coils of clammy mist that made it hard to choose direction. Kirk hesitated.

"I think we bear left," he said. But the turn they took led them into an alley. They had paused, about to retrace their steps, when a woman's agonized scream tore the silent darkness before them. "It came from there!" Kirk shouted, and plunged deeper into the foggy alley, McCoy at his heels. They both stopped at the sound of heavy breathing. Kirk took a forward step only to stop again. He had stumbled over a body.

It was sprawled, face down, on the damp paving. The back of the cloak it wore was ripped by venomous slashes.

McCoy, kneeling beside it, lifted the head. After a long moment, he raised a face that was blanched with horror. "It's Kara," he said. "Dead. Stabbed a dozen times."

The heavy breathing sound came again. They ran toward it. Scott was crouched against the alley wall. He stared at them unseeingly, his face twisted into a grimace. In his hands he held a long, sharp knife. It was wet with blood.

The café had got rid of its customers, and bright lights had replaced its dimness. Unspeaking, Kirk and McCoy stood beside the table where Scott sat, huddled, his face in his hands. Like Scott, they made no move when the pudgy, round-faced man who faced them said, "Argelius is the last planet in the galaxy where I'd expect a thing like this to happen. I'm at a loss to explain it, gentlemen."

"We are just as shocked as you are, Mr. Hengist," Kirk assured him.

"If this were my home planet, Rigel IV," Hengist was saying, "I'd have a dozen investigators at my disposal as Chief City Administrator. But they don't exist here."

"Then you are not a native Argelian, sir?" McCoy asked.

"No. Argelius hires its administrative officers from other planets. Its people's virtue is gentleness, not efficiency."

"You can count," Kirk told him, "on our complete cooperation. We will conduct ourselves according to your local laws."

"That's the trouble," Hengist frowned. "There are no laws to deal with a thing like this. Ancient traditions, of course, dating back before the great Argelian Awakening. But they're rather barbaric. I can't be expected to put your Mr. Scott to torture."

"We might be able to help," Kirk suggested. "We have equipment on the *Enterprise* which would help us get at the facts."

Hengist shook his head. "That's quite impossible, Captain, quite impossible. The investigation must take place here."

He picked up the murder knife from the table, looking down at the broken figure of Scott. "Mr. Scott—Mr. Scott, kindly rouse yourself! Are you sure you've never seen this knife before?"

Scott stared, dull-eyed, at the knife.

Kirk spoke sharply. "Answer him, Scott!"

"I—don't remember," Scott said.

Hengist made a gesture of impatience. He looked at Kirk. "You can scarcely call that helpful, Captain!"

Kirk pulled up a chair beside Scott. "Scotty," he said quietly, "you left the café with the girl. You remember that, don't you? What happened next?"

The dull eyes turned to him. "We were walking—the fog. I was ahead of her, trying to lead the way. Then—

then I heard her scream. I remember starting to turn—"

His face contorted. Then words burst out of him. "I can't remember another thing!"

Beckoning to McCoy, Kirk got up from the chair. "Well, Bones?" he said.

"If he says he can't remember, he probably doesn't. You know Scotty."

"I also know a murder has been committed—and that we found him with a bloody knife in his hand."

"That proves nothing," McCoy said. "Surely you don't think . . ."

"What *I* think doesn't make any difference! We're guests here! A member of my crew is under suspicion!"

"But you don't throw him to the wolves!" cried McCoy.

"I've got a diplomatic responsibility, Bones. This happened under Argelian jurisdiction. If they want to arrest Scotty, put him through trial here—even convict him, I've got to go along with them." He paused. "Besides, this business of not remembering . . ."

"Jim, he's just recovering from a very severe concussion! Partial amnesia after a thing like that is not only possible, it's probable. Especially under great stress."

"It's out of my hands, Bones. We'll do all that we can—but only under Argelian laws. There's Hengist at him again. Let's get back."

The pudgy man had replaced the knife on the table. "Not very promising, Captain Kirk. Your man still insists he remembers nothing. But my detector readings show his fingerprints on the murder weapon."

"Mr. Hengist," said Kirk, "other people left this café at about the same time Mr. Scott and the girl did."

"So I've been told by the staff. Those people will be located and questioned. But the outlook for your friend is pretty grim. I'm a man who prides himself on doing his job well. This crime will be solved and its perpetrator punished!"

"What is the law in such cases, Mr. Hengist?"

A deep voice spoke. "The Law of Argelius, sir, is love."

Kirk turned. A tall, white-haired, distinguished man

had entered the café. A woman, almost as tall, was with him. Slim, elegant, her black hair touched with gray at the temples, the quiet gravity of her composure was impressive. Hengist bowed deeply to them both.

"Gentlemen," he said, "our Prefect—Jaris. Sir, Captain Kirk and Dr. McCoy."

Presenting the beautiful woman, Jaris said, "My wife, Sybo."

She inclined her head. "And this man at the table is Scott," Hengist said. "The one I told you about in my message."

Jaris's tranquil eyes studied Scott's face. "He does not look like a man capable of murder. Still, it has been so long since—" The deep voice spoke to Kirk and McCoy. "Gentlemen, before our great awakening hundreds of years ago, we had ways of learning the truth in such matters. We will return to them."

"The Argelian empathic contact, sir?" McCoy said.

"You know of it, Doctor?"

"I've heard of it. I had assumed it was a lost art."

"My wife is a descendant of the ancient priestesses of our land," Jaris said. "She has the old gift. I have come to invite you all to my home."

Hengist protested. "Prefect, don't you think this should be handled in an official manner through my office?"

"It *shall* be handled in an official manner, inasmuch as I am the highest official of Argelius." The rebuke was as gently spoken as it was courteous. "We will now proceed to my home. There my wife will prepare herself—and we shall learn the truth. Sybo—" He stood aside, bowing, and she moved past him to the café door.

Her drawing room was as impressive as their hostess. It was high-ceilinged, circular and windowless. Luxurious draperies covered its exits. Its tables, chairs, its cabinets matched the draperies in taste. Against one wall there was a simple altar of rich wood. A single flame rose from it.

"I have informed my ship, sir," Kirk turned to Jaris, "that there will be a delay in our return."

"Well done, Captain." Jaris nodded. "Let us proceed. Pray be seated, everyone."

McCoy was restive. "Prefect, depending on your lovely wife's empathic abilities is all very well. But I am a scientist, sir. And my science has available a precise method by which we can discover what it is that Mr. Scott cannot remember. Since you won't permit us to go to our ship, I can beam down a technician with my psychotricorder. It will give us a detailed account of all that has happened to Mr. Scott within the past twenty-four hours."

"I advise against it, Prefect," Hengist said. "This is a purely Argelian matter."

"My wife must meditate for a time before she is ready," Jaris told him. "I see no reason why we should not employ that time to all possible use. Very well, Dr. McCoy."

McCoy whipped out his communicator. "McCoy to *Enterprise*."

"Spock here, Doctor."

"Mr. Spock, please beam down a technician with a psychotricorder immediately. Use these coordinates."

"Acknowledged. Coordinates received and read," Spock answered.

"Thanks. McCoy out."

Jaris was confiding his own problems to Kirk. "News of this frightful event is spreading among our people. They are greatly disturbed. Already there is talk of placing Argelius under embargo to space vehicles."

"That would be most unfortunate, sir. Argelius is widely known for its hospitality. It also owns strategic importance as a spaceport. It is the only one in this quadrant."

"Prefect," McCoy intervened, "the tricorder examination will require privacy to be effective."

"There is a small chamber below this room. Perhaps it will suffice, Doctor."

Hengist rose from his chair. "I do not wish to seem argumentative, Prefect, but I must point out that these two gentlemen are Mr. Scott's friends. They *want* to clear him!"

"And if he is innocent, do you not want to clear him, too, Mr. Hengist?"

The mild question rattled Hengist. "Why—I—of course," he stammered. "I am only interested in the truth."

"So are we all," said Kirk brusquely.

The flustered City Administrator addressed Jaris. "There are other people to be questioned. Perhaps I should go to expedite their arrival here."

"Please do so," said the Prefect. "Anyone who has any connection with the murder should be here during the ceremony."

But Hengist's departure was delayed by the Transporter dazzle that appeared near McCoy's chair. It gradually assumed the extremely attractive shape and features of crewwoman Karen Tracy. Hengist eyed her. Then, nodding to her, he passed her and disappeared through a draped door.

The girl, a psychotricorder slung over her shoulder, said, "Lieutenant Karen Tracy, Doctor, reporting as ordered."

Scott, dismay in his face, half-rose from his chair. "A—a woman," he mumbled.

Kirk saw Jaris's keen eyes fix on him. "You don't like women, Mr. Scott?"

"It's not that, Prefect," McCoy said quickly. "He was recently involved in an accident caused by a careless woman. He suffered a severe concussion."

"Damage to his brain, Doctor?"

"Some. But in my best opinion, it could not possibly be responsible for. . ."

"I suggested nothing, Doctor."

"No. Of course you didn't." McCoy made a visible effort to get his anxiety back under control. "Lieutenant, I want a twenty-four-hour regressive memory check on Mr. Scott. All possible amnesic gaps to be probed."

"Yes, Doctor. Where shall I set up?"

"If you will follow me, young lady—" Jaris was leading the way toward the room's nearest exit when Kirk spoke to Scott. "You are to give Lieutenant Tracy complete cooperation. Maybe we can clear this thing up once and for all."

At the look in Scott's eyes, Kirk had to down an impulse to place an encouraging hand on his shoulder. "Yes, Captain. This—not remembering—it's hard to take."

Kirk watched him go with Tracy and Jaris. "All right, Bones. We're alone. Opinions?"

McCoy was grave. "Jim, in normal circumstances, Scotty simply couldn't have done such a thing. But that knock on the head—it could have tossed all his previous behavior patterns into a junk heap. What worries me is that he's telling the truth about not remembering."

"Why does it worry you?"

"Hysterical amnesia. When a man feels guilt about something—something too terrible to face up to—he will blot it out of his conscious memory."

Kirk felt his mind wince away from the words. Was it possible that Scott's conscious memory was sparing him recollection of an action too appalling to remember? The windowless room seemed suddenly suffocating. I need fresh air, he thought—but Jaris had returned. And the slender Sybo, her face absent-looking, abstracted, was pushing aside the drapery of another door.

"Are you prepared, Sybo?" Jaris asked her.

"I am ready. May I have the knife, please?"

Jaris turned to them. "My wife also possesses the ability to receive sensory impressions from inanimate objects." He moved to a table. "The knife," he said. "Do you have it, Captain?"

Startled, Kirk echoed, "The knife? No. I thought . . ."

"I placed it on this table when we arrived," Jaris said. "It's gone."

There was an uncomfortable silence. It was shattered by a shriek, muffled, but so high-pitched that it penetrated the floor's tiling. The underground room! Kirk and McCoy exchanged the same glance of apprehension. Then Kirk burst into action. Tearing aside a door curtain, he bolted headlong down a flight of stairs, McCoy's feet pounding behind him. They were in an

ill-lit hall, a closed door facing them. Kirk broke
through it into a small chamber.

Scott, his eyes closed, was sitting, rigid, in a chair.
Karen Tracy, her equipment scattered around her, lay
on the floor. McCoy ran to her. But Kirk had seized
Scott's shoulder. "Scotty!" he shouted, shaking the
shoulder. "Scotty, snap out of it!"

The shoulder sagged under his hand. Scott moaned,
swaying, while McCoy, getting to his feet, said, "She's
dead, Jim."

Kirk looked at him. "Don't tell me. I know," he
said. "She's been stabbed to death, hasn't she?"

"Over and over again," McCoy said. "Just like the
other one."

They had to support Scott up the stairs. Jaris poured
some amber fluid into a glass and handed it to McCoy.
"An Argelian stimulant, Doctor. An effective one." But
an overwhelming tension had reclaimed Scott. The glass
just clattered against his clenched teeth. It took the
combined skills of McCoy and Kirk to pry his locked
jaws open and pour the liquid down his throat. As
color began to return to his ashen lips, Kirk saw that
Sybo had stepped to the altar, a dream-lost look on her
face. A nice thing to have—a private dream world, he
thought grimly, pouring the rest of the liquor into
Scott's mouth. This time he swallowed it voluntarily.
Blinking his eyes, he glanced around him. "Lieutenant
Tracy?" he said. "Captain—where is . . .?"

"Lieutenant Tracy is dead," Kirk said.

Scott stared at him. "Dead?"

"Yes," Kirk said harshly. "What happened down
there?"

"I was sitting there, sir—and she was taking the
readings." He made a move to rise. "Why am I back
here now? She wasn't finished."

"That's all you remember?" McCoy asked.

"Scott, *concentrate!*" Kirk said. "The girl is dead.
You were with her. You must have seen what happened. What was it?"

The anguished look of helplessness returned to
Scott's eyes. "I don't remember. I can't remember,

Captain. I must have passed out, but why, if I did . . ."

McCoy said, "It could be, Jim. The head injury . . ."

Kirk yelled, "I don't want to hear any more about that head injury! Scott! *Think!*"

"Watch it, Jim," McCoy said. "If he can't think, he can't do it because he's told to."

Kirk swung around to Jaris. "Prefect, is there another door to that room?"

"One that leads into the garden. But it's been locked for years."

"Locks can be picked," McCoy remarked.

"Check it, Bones," Kirk said.

Somewhere a bell rang. Jaris pressed a button, and Hengist, shoving two men before him, pushed through a door curtain. "Prefect," he said, "both of these people were in that café the night of the murder."

Kirk spoke to the older man. "I've seen you. You were one of the café's musicians. You played for Kara."

"She was my daughter," the man said. "She danced to my music as a child. Now she is dead and I am left to grieve." He turned to Jaris. "Prefect, how could this thing happen here? The man who did it must be found. And punished."

Hengist said, "I promise he will be, Tark."

Kirk indicated the younger man. "And *he* left the café just before Scott and Kara."

"Who are you?" Jaris asked the man. "Is what you have just heard true?"

"I am Morla of Cantaba Street. Yes, Prefect. I was there. I have nothing to hide."

"Did you know Kara?" Kirk asked.

Morla nodded. And Tark cried, "Of course he knew her! They were to be married. But his jealousy was a disgust to my child!"

"Jealousy?" Jaris said. "That is disquieting. In Argelius jealousy is virtually unknown."

Morla's mouth trembled. "My jealousy was a sorrow to me, Prefect. But I could not help it. I loved her. When I saw her go to the table with these men, I could not watch. I left the café."

"Where did you go?" Kirk asked.

"Home. Straight to my home. I needed to meditate—to rid myself of anger."

Kirk said, "Prefect, jealousy is a notorious reason for murder."

"I know. That is why it is disapproved here."

"I could not kill." Morla's voice broke. "It is not in me to kill. It is not in me to kill what I loved."

McCoy, returning, took in the scene. "That lock may or may not have been picked, Jim. Even with a tricorder, it would be hard to tell."

Kirk spoke again to Morla. "Can you prove that you went straight home?"

Hengist broke in. "Captain, I insist that you leave this questioning to me!"

"Then get on with it, man!" Kirk shouted. "Don't just hang around!" He looked at Tark. "A father, maybe angered by a daughter's disobedience—you wouldn't be the first one to—" He broke off. "Prefect! A future husband enraged at seeing his girl with other men—you cannot deny that is motive for murder! But Mr. Scott had none. Lieutenant Tracy was killed because she was about to discover the truth!"

Jaris's reply came slowly. "That is possible, Captain."

"Probable, sir."

The mild eyes met Kirk's. "Captain, you sound, you know, like a man who's determined to save the life of a friend."

"Yes, sir. Your judgment of me is impeccable. I *do* want to save my friend. And I remind you that he has not yet been proven guilty."

"Let me remind *you* that this friend of yours has been found with the body in each of these cases." Hengist's round face had flushed with anger.

Kirk had no time for a further retort, because at that moment Sybo announced, "I am ready, husband."

There was a strange authority in her quiet voice. Nobody spoke as she turned from the altar, her face serene, reposed. "The flame of purification burns," she said. "It points to the direction of truth." She stepped down from the altar. "We shall join hands. Our minds shall mingle—and I shall look into your deep hearts."

With a courtly gesture, Jaris led her to the table. "We shall sit, gentlemen, all of us. And as my wife asks, we shall join hands."

"On one condition, sir," Kirk said. "This room must be sealed so no one can enter or leave it during the ritual."

"The room *is* sealed," Jaris said.

He was seating Sybo at the table when Kirk's communicator beeped. It was Spock. "May I have a word with you, Captain?"

Kirk turned to Jaris. "A message from my ship, sir. Please excuse me for a moment." He moved to the end of the room. "Yes, Mr. Spock?"

"I have been considering the unfortunate situation, sir, as you related it to us. In my opinion, the Argelian empathic contact is a phenomenon worthy of study. I merely wonder if it is sound enough a technique to entrust with a man's life."

"What do you suggest, Mr. Spock?"

"That we beam up Mr. Scott in order to allow our computers to arrive at the truth."

"Impractical, Mr. Spock. To adopt your suggestion could close Argelius as a spaceport. We must respect the emotions and pride of these people. They have their own methods for handling this affair—and while we are here, we are subject to them."

"Understood, Captain."

"I don't like it any more than you do; but there's nothing we can do about it. Kirk out."

When he faced the room again, everyone was seated at the table, Sybo at its head. Behind her the altar flame flared up—and waned. "Let us begin," she said. "Let us join hands. Let the circle not be broken. Look upon the fire that burns on the altar of truth."

Her eyes closed. The odd authority in her low voice now invested her stillness. Kirk saw her lift a rapt face, the room putting shadow into the hollows beneath her cheekbones. Then suddenly, shockingly, she was speaking in a different voice—a much older voice, deeper, resonant. "Yes, there is something here in this room— something terrible—out of the past. I feel its pres-

ence—fear, rage, hatred." A groan broke from her.
"There is evil here—monstrous, demonic . . ."

She paused as though all her senses were centered on
listening. "A consuming hunger that never dies—hatred
of life, of woman, hatred undying." The voice rose. "It
is strong—an ancient hunger that feeds on terror—
closer, closer—growing among us now—evil lust for
death—death. It has been named—boratis—kesla—
redjac . . ."

Sybo's words were coming in a frightened wail. "Devouring evil—eating life, light—hunger that preys—
redjac—redjac . . ."

The altar flame winked out. In the darkness flooding
the room, Kirk heard a rushing sound like the flapping
of great wings. Then Sybo gave a wild scream.

"Get the lights!" he shouted.

They blazed up. Hengist was over at the light panel,
his hand still on it.

But all Kirk had eyes for was Sybo. She was slumped
in Scott's arms. Very slowly her body twisted in them.
From her back the haft of a long knife protruded.
Scott's nerveless arms relaxed—and the body fell to the
floor. Scott looked down at it. Then Kirk saw him look
away from it to stare at his bloody hands.

Jaris's face was gaunt with grief. And Kirk, listening
to Hengist's tirade, thought—and not for the first time—
Mr. City Administrator, you are an insensitive man.

"Three murders!" Hengist was yelling. "And this
man on the scene each time! What do you require,
Captain? That he stab another woman in the back
before your very eyes?"

"Mr. Hengist, please—not now," Jaris said. "My
poor wife—her body has just been removed . . ."

Hengist persisted. "Prefect, I am perfectly satisfied
that this *Enterprise* crewman is guilty!"

"But not responsible," Kirk said. "These acts have
been acts of insanity. If Mr. Scott is guilty, he is a
madman. On our ship we have instruments able to
determine his mental state."

"And save his life?" There was a sneer in Hengist's
voice.

"Insanity cannot be held responsible under anybody's laws," Kirk said. "It is unaware of what it does to others."

"Gentlemen, please—" Jaris said.

"I am sorry, Prefect," Hengist said. "My heart grieves for you—but I can stand by no longer! This man has killed three times! Even Captain Kirk admits it! But this last-minute attempt to help Scott evade punishment. . . ."

Kirk kept his voice level. "No, Mr. Hengist. To see that justice is done."

"I—don't know," Jaris said.

"How many other murders will occur unless we take prompt action, sir?" Hengist asked him. "The old laws still exist. I can get the truth from this killer."

"By torture?" Kirk said. He turned to Jaris. "Prefect, I told you before, we'll stand by your laws. If Mr. Scott is mentally responsible, he is yours to punish. But I must insist that everything possible be done to establish his mental condition."

Jaris's mouth trembled. Shock had visibly aged him. "How could any man do these monstrous things?"

"That is what I hope to find out, sir," Kirk said gently.

With an effort Jaris looked at Scott. "And you, Mr. Scott, what do you have to say?"

Scott stood up. "Sir, I swear before God that I did not kill your wife. I have not killed anyone."

"By your own admission you don't know whether you did or not," Hengist said. "Your so-called failure of memory . . ."

"Mr. Hengist," McCoy interrupted him, "aboard our ship it is possible to record all registrations that have been made on Mr. Scott's conscious or subconscious mind. We can recover all that has occurred to him. The recordings are factual. They will tell us exactly what has happened to him in the recent past."

Kirk pressed McCoy's point. "There would be no room for doubt," he said. "We would *know*. Isn't that what we want, Prefect? To *know*?" He looked at Hengist. "The investigation and disposition of the case would still remain in your jurisdiction. *What we're after is the removal of doubts.*"

Hengist's face hardened. "Your suggestion would be illegal. If this man is taken back into your ship with you, what legal assurance do we have you'd return him to Argelius even if your instruments prove him guilty? I have the authority to . . ."

Jaris had recovered control of himself. "Mr. Hengist, the authority is mine," he said firmly. "And this decision, too, is mine." He looked at Kirk. "Captain, as you know, Mr. Scott has claimed to remember nothing about the murders. He may have killed without knowing he killed. Can your machines penetrate to the truth of his actions?"

"They will so correlate the facts that a positive conclusion is reached," Kirk said. "No doubts will remain."

Jaris rose. "Very well. We shall go to your ship."

He walked over to Scott, his step steady. "If you are guilty," he said, "you will face the ancient penalties, barbaric though they may be. I warn you that the ancient penalty for murder was death by slow torture. That law has never been changed. Do you understand, Mr. Scott?"

Scott moistened his dry lips. But he faced Jaris unflinchingly. "Aye, sir. I understand."

The Briefing Room of the *Enterprise* was crowded. The Argelian guests, including Tark and Morla, had been seated on one side of its table. On the other side, a pretty yeoman, Tancris, sat between Scott and McCoy, prepared to record the proceedings. Kirk with Spock stood near the computer controls.

Kirk addressed his guests. "Deep in the heart of this ship are our computer banks. They operate the entire ship. They also contain the whole of human and humanoid knowledge. They are indisputably reliable. Our lives depend on them."

He turned to Spock. "Anything to add, Mr. Spock?"

"In a matter of a few seconds," Spock said, "we can obtain an answer to any factual question, regardless of its complexity."

"You don't solve a murder with columns of figures!" Hengist said.

"No, sir. But we do determine the truth."

"How?" asked Morla. "That machine can't tell what goes on in a man's mind!"

Kirk pointed to the computer's verifier. "No. But this piece of equipment can—to an extent." He pulled out a chair. "Each testifier will sit here, his hand on this plate. Any deviation from factual truth will be immediately detected. It will then be relayed to the computer which will notify us."

Hengist stirred in his chair. Kirk continued. "Doctor McCoy has already fed his medical reports into the computer. Our laboratory experts are now examining the murder weapon. They will give their findings to the computer for its analysis. Mr. Scott, will you please take the stand?"

Scott rose, moved to the verifier, sat down and laid his hand on the plate. Kirk activated the computer control.

"Computer," he said. "Identify and verify."

The mechanism clicked. And the computer voice spoke. "Working. Lieutenant Commander Montgomery Scott, serial number SE 197–547–230T. Verified."

"Subject's present physical condition?" Kirk said.

"Working. Subject recently subjected to severe blow on skull. Damage healing. Some peripheral abnormalities."

"Sufficient abnormalities to cause periods of functional amnesia?"

"Working," responded the computer. "Negative."

Puzzled, McCoy intervened. "I don't see how that can be, Jim."

"It can be if Scotty is lying about his loss of memory," Kirk said.

"I'm not lying, Captain!" Scott cried. "I don't remember a thing about the first two murders!"

"Computer. Accuracy scan," said Kirk.

"Subject relaying accurate account. No physiological changes."

Scott, his hand still on the plate, half-rose from the

chair. "Captain, I never said I blacked out when the Prefect's wife was killed!"

"All right, Scott. Go ahead. What do you remember about it?"

"We were all holding hands. The room was dark, the light from the altar was so dim. I heard the poor lady scream. I tried to reach her—but something was between us."

"Something?" Kirk questioned. "You mean someone?"

"No, sir. Some—thing. Cold—it was cold like a stinking draft out of a slaughterhouse. But—it wasn't really there like—" He stopped, adding lamely, "If you get what I mean."

"Computer?" Kirk said.

"Subject relaying accurate account. No physiological changes."

"All right," said Kirk. "I'm putting it straight. Scott, did you kill Sybo?"

"No, sir. That I'm sure of."

Hengist grunted. "He's been saying that all along. It means no more now than it did before."

Kirk eyed him. "Scotty!" he said. "Lie to me! How old are you?"

"Twenty-two, Captain."

A buzzer sounded. The touch panel blinked a light on and off. And the computer voice said, "Inaccurate. Inaccurate. Data in error."

"Scott, when the lights went out, who was holding your hand?"

"Morla on the one side, sir—you on the other."

Morla, his face pale, got to his feet. "But that doesn't mean anything, Captain. A small room like that—it was dark—anyone of us would have had time to kill the lady."

Hengist was quick to object. "I remind everyone we found Mr. Scott holding her in his arms. The knife was still in her back. And there was blood on his hands."

"That is so," Kirk said. "But the verifier has shown it will accept no lie."

"Two other women were murdered," Hengist challenged.

"Mr. Scott," Kirk said, "did you kill Kara?"

"I don't remember."

"Did you kill Lieutenant Tracy?"

"I can't remember."

"Computer," Kirk said. "Accuracy scan."

"Subject relaying accurate account. No physiological changes."

"All this proves," Jaris said, "is that he's telling the truth about the memory lapses."

"It's a waste of our time!" Hengist exclaimed.

Kirk said, "Mr. Hengist, after this testimony is taken, we will run a psychotricorder analysis of Mr. Scott's memory. That's what Lieutenant Tracy was trying to do. This time we'll do it. We shall have a complete record of the action he took, remembered or forgotten. Will that satisfy you?"

"If you can convince me that the machine is incapable of error. If it shows that he did not kill the women."

"The machine does not err. As to the rest of it, the readings will reveal that. I think you can stand down, Mr. Scott—if there are no objections."

"I object to this entire procedure!" Hengist shouted.

Mildly, Jaris turned to him. "Mr. Hengist, we are here on my authority."

"Prefect, I know you mean well—but I have had past experience in matters of this kind while you . . ."

"Enough, sir," Jaris stopped him short. "For the present we will accept Captain Kirk's trust of the machine's accuracy. At the same time we'll reserve the right to make the final determination ourselves."

"That's all we ask, Prefect," Kirk said. "Mr. Morla, will you take the stand?"

Morla took it, placing his hand nervously on the touch plate, and Kirk said, "Where were you at the time Kara was murdered?"

"I—I'm not sure. Walking home, I think. I was disturbed." He looked at Kirk. "I told you I felt anger."

"Anger is a relative state, Mr. Morla," interposed Spock. "Were you angry enough to do violence?"

"I have never done violence in my life. I am an

Argelian. I do not believe I am capable of violence."
His voice shook. "Believe me, I couldn't kill her! She
loved me!"

Tark jumped to his feet. "That is not true! She did
not love him! She told me. He was jealous! They fought
constantly!" Tears in his eyes, he turned to Jaris. "My
daughter was a true Argelian. A child of joy . . ."

"Yes, I *was* jealous!" Morla was on his feet, too. "I
admit it! But I did not kill her! I wanted to leave
Argelius with her—go somewhere to have her all to
myself. I loved her!"

"Did you kill Lieutenant Tracy?" Kirk asked.

"No!"

"Did you kill Sybo?"

"No!"

"Computer—verification scan," Kirk said.

"Subject relaying accurate account. Some statements
subjective. No physiological changes."

"That would seem to be it," Kirk said. "You can
stand down, Mr. Morla."

"He glanced around the faces at the table. After a
long moment, he said slowly, "Sybo spoke of a consuming hunger that never dies—of something that
thrives on terror, on death." He looked at Spock.
"Maybe we're going about this the wrong way. Let's
assume that Sybo was a sensitive—that she *did* sense
something evil in that room . . ."

"The sensitivity of certain Argelian women is a
documented fact, Captain," Spock said.

"My—dear wife's talent," said Jaris, "was genuine,
gentlemen. The things she said were true."

"All right, then," said Kirk. "Exactly what was it she
said? A monstrous evil—out of the past—hatred of
life, of woman . . ."

"A lust for death," supplemented McCoy.

"She made some other references that didn't make
sense," Kirk said.

"I remember them," McCoy told him. "Redjac. Boratis. Kesla."

Kirk shook his head. "Obscure. Meaningless."

"To us, perhaps, Captain," Spock said. "But to the
computer banks . . ."

"Check them out, Mr. Spock."

"Computer, linguistic banks," Spock said. "Definition of following word—redjac."

The computer buzzed. "Working. Negative finding."

"There's no such word in the linguistic bank?"

"Affirmative."

"Scan all other banks," Spock said.

"Working. Affirmative. A proper name."

"Define," Spock said.

"Working. Red Jack. Source: Earth, nineteenth century. Language: English. Nickname applied to mass murderer of women. Other Earth synonym: Jack the Ripper."

A silence composed of shock, hope and incredulity fell over the listeners.

"That's ridiculous!" Hengist yelled. He leaped to his feet. "Jack the Ripper lived hundreds of years ago!"

Kirk said, "Computer. Factual data and capsulization on Jack the Ripper."

"Working. Jack the Ripper: First appearance, London, ancient British Empire, Earth, year 1888, old calendar. Brutal killer of at least six women by knife or surgical instrument; no witnesses to crimes; no identification or arrest. Crimes remain unsolved. No known motive."

"Senseless crimes," McCoy said reflectively.

"As senseless as the murder of Kara—or Lieutenant Tracy," said Kirk.

Tark looked from one to the other. "It can't be. A man could not survive all these centuries."

"My wife," Jaris said. "My wife—before she died—it is a deathless hunger, she said."

"But all men die!" protested Tark.

"All *men* die, sir," Spock said. "But humans and humanoids comprise only a small percent of the life forms we know of. There exist entities possessed of extremely long life-spans, virtually immortal."

"But—a being which feeds on death?" McCoy shook his head.

"In the strict scientific sense, Doctor, we all live on death—even vegetarians."

"But Sybo said it feeds on terror!"

"Deriving sustenance from emotion is not unknown—and fear is among the strongest and most intense of the emotions."

Hengist's eyes lingered on Spock's quiet face. Then he swung around to Jaris. "Prefect, this has gone far enough! Someone, some man has killed three women. We have the prime suspect in our hands! Are we going to let him go to chase down ghosts?"

"Not ghosts, Mr. Hengist," Kirk said. "Possibly not human—but not a ghost. Mr. Spock, run a check on the possibilities."

"Computer. Digest log recordings of past five solar minutes. Correlate hypotheses. Compare with life forms register. Question: could such an entity within discussed limits, exist in this galaxy?"

"Affirmative. Examples exist. The Drella of Alpha Carinae V derives its sustenance from the emotion of love. There exists sufficient precedent for existence of creature, nature unknown, which could exist on emotion of terror."

"Extrapolate most likely composition of such entity," Spock said.

"Working. To meet specified requirements, entity would exist without form in conventional sense. Most probable: mass of energy, highly cohesive."

Kirk took over. "Computer, in such form, could the entity kill with a knife?"

"Negative."

"Could the entity described assume physical form?"

"Affirmative. Precedent: the Mellitus, cloud creature of Alpha Majoris 1."

"Fairy tales!" Hengist was acid with scorn. "Ghosts and goblins!"

Kirk was getting his fill of Hengist. "No, sir," he said. "I've seen the Mellitus myself. Its normal state is gaseous but at rest it becomes solid." He turned back to Spock. "Let's assume the existence of this creature able to take on form or reject it at will. That could explain Scotty's failure to remember anything about the first two murders."

Spock nodded. "Or by production of a hypnotic

screen blinding all but the victim to the killer's presence."

Awed, Jaris murmured, "Is that possible?"

"Very possible," McCoy told him. "Even probable. Many examples exist in nature."

"But I don't hypnotize easily," Scott interjected.

"We're not talking about a human hypnotist, Scotty," Kirk reminded him.

Hengist, openly furious, rose again from the table. "This is fantasy! We all know the murderer is sitting right here with us! You're trying to muddy the issue. I've got a mind to stop this right now!"

"Kindly be seated, Mr. Hengist." Jaris sounded unusually stern. "The course of this investigation seems valid to me."

Conscious of the glaring Hengist behind him, Kirk said, "What do we have then, Mr. Spock? A creature without stable form that feeds on fear, assuming physical shape to do its killing?"

"And preys on women because they are more easily terrorized than the male of the species."

Kirk hit the computer button. "Computer, criminological files. Cases of unsolved multiple murders of women since Jack the Ripper."

"Working. 1932. Shanghai, China, Earth. Seven women knifed to death. 1974. Kiev, USSR, Earth. Five women knifed to death. 2005. Martian Colonies. Eight women knifed to death. Heliopolis, Alpha Proximi II. Ten women knifed to death. There are additional examples."

"Captain," Spock said, "all those places are aligned directly between Argelius and Earth."

"Yes. When men of Earth moved into the galaxy, this thing must have moved with them." He addressed the computer. "Identify the proper names Kesla and Boratis."

"Working. Kesla: popular name of unidentified mass murderer of women on planet Deneb II. Boratis: popular name of unidentified mass murderer of women on planet Rigel IV. Additional data. Murders on Rigel IV occurred one solar year ago."

McCoy turned from the table to look at Kirk. Kirk,

nodding, spoke to Hengist. "You came to Argelius from Rigel IV," he said.

"Many people do," Hengist countered, "It's not a crime."

"No. But we are investigating one. Please take the stand, Mr. Hengist."

Hengist leaned back in his chair. "I refuse," he said.

"Mr. Hengist!"

The jaw in the pudgy face had set hard. "Prefect, I will *not* take the stand."

"I see your point, sir," Spock said. "If you are the entity we search for, what better hiding place could you find than the official position you hold?"

McCoy was on his feet. "And just after you left Jaris's house, we discovered the murder weapon was missing!"

Kirk pressed on. "You were unaccounted for when Lieutenant Tracy was murdered."

A nerve under Hengist's eye twitched. "The law is my business!" His voice roughened. "You are engaged in sheer speculation for your own illegal ends!"

Kirk was not deferred. "Mr. Spock—the weapon."

"Computer," Spock said. "Report on analysis of Exhibit A."

"Working. Exhibit A on visual."

The mechanism's triscreen flashed into brightness. As the image of the knife appeared on it, its voice said, "Composition of blade: boridium. Composition of handle: murinite. Details of handle carving conform to folk art indicating place of origin."

"Specify place of origin," Spock said.

"Artifact produced by hill people of Argus River region, planet Rigel IV."

"Mr. Hengist—" Kirk began.

But Hengist had made a break for the door. Scott tripped him—and Kirk closed with him. There was unexpected muscle in the pudgy body. Screaming wildly, Hengist aimed a knee at Kirk's groin. Elbowing up, Kirk swung a fist back and landed a hard right to his jaw. Hengist collapsed. The lights went dim; and at the same moment the room was filled with that rushing sound like the flapping of great wings.

Kirk got to his feet. McCoy, looking up from Hengist's body, said tonelessly, "He's dead, Jim."

"Dead? But that's impossible! A man doesn't die of a sock on the jaw!"

The computer crackled. Then the noise subsided. A maniacal laughter burst from its speakers. They chuckled, choking with obscene merriment—and Hengist's voice shrieked, "Red Jack! Red Jack! Red Jack!"

The cackling mirth grew into an insane howl of triumph. Kirk, astounded, stared at Spock. The Vulcan leaped to the computer buttons. But the mad howls of laughter would not be stilled.

"The computer isn't responding, Captain! The entity has taken possession of it!"

"But the computer controls the ship!" Kirk cried. "Are you saying that this thing is in possession of the ship?"

He himself began to wrestle with the computer controls. Spock tried to move the switch that fed into its bypass circuits. It swung loose. "It's no use, Captain! The bypass circuits have been blocked, too!"

The crazy laughter gushed louder from the speakers. "Red Jack!" it screamed again.

"Audio cutoff, Mr. Spock!"

The room was suddenly quiet. But Scott, jumping to his feet, yelled, "The screen, Captain! Look at the screen!"

Kirk whirled. The viewer was a riot of changing colors. Figures began to emerge from them. Serpents writhed through pentagons. Naked women, hair streaming behind them, rode astride the shaggy backs of goats. Horned beasts pranced with toads. Rivers boiled, steaming. Above them, embraced bodies drifted down fiery winds. Human shoulders, pinioned under rocks, lifted pleading arms. Then the red glow, shedding its bloody mist over the screen, gave way to the deathly whiteness of a cold, unending snow. Up from the glacial landscape rose a towering three-headed shape, its mouths agape with gusts of silent laughter. A cross, upturned, appeared beside it. The shape crawled up it, suspending itself upon it in an unspeakable travesty of the crucifixion. Its vast, leathery wings unfolded . . .

"What is it?" Jaris whispered.

"A vision of hell," Kirk said. He switched off the screen. "This foul thing has shown us the place of its origin. And it is now master of all this ship's operations, including our life support systems."

"You mean it could kill us all?" gasped Morla.

"I suspect it will try," Spock said. "But not immediately." He paused. "It feeds on terror. Death is not enough for it. There are nearly four hundred and forty humans aboard this ship. They offer it an unparalleled opportunity to glut itself on the fear it can stimulate in them. Before it kills, it will make the most of its chance."

Kirk nodded. He moved over to the intercom button. Pressing it, he said, "All hands, this is the Captain speaking. The computers are malfunctioning. Repair efforts are proceeding. Meanwhile, it is of the utmost importance to stay at your posts and remain calm. Captain out."

He faced around. "Bones, what's your sedative situation?"

"I've got some stuff that would tranquilize a volcano, Jim."

"Start distributing it to all hands. The longer we can hold fear down, the more time we'll have to get this hell-born thing out of the computers."

He swung back to Spock. "Mr. Spock, you have a compulsory scan order built into your computer control banks."

"Yes, Captain, but with the entity in control . . ."

"Even so, it will have to deal with everything programmed into the computers. Aren't there some mathematical problems which simply cannot be solved?"

Spock's somber face lightened. "Indeed there are, Captain. If we can focus all the computers' attention on one of them . . ."

"Good. That should do it." Kirk moved over to the table. "The rest of you, stay here," he said. "Bones, get going on that tranquilizer. Let's go, Mr. Spock."

But the thing had taken over the elevator. Though its door slid open to admit Kirk, it started to slam shut before Spock could enter it. "Spock!" Kirk shouted. He grabbed him, yanking him in just as the door clanged shut. Spock turned to regard the door with interest. "Fascinating," he said. "Our friend learns quickly."

"Too quickly." Kirk pushed the up button to the bridge. Instead of rising, the elevator sank. Decks flashed by to a whining sound. "Free fall!" Kirk yelled. "Put it on manual control!"

They both seized the manual controls, pulling at them. The whine stopped, and very slowly the elevator began to rise. Then its alarm siren shrieked. "That was due to be next," Kirk said grimly. "Life support malfunction!"

"We don't have much time, Captain."

"You said it yourself, Mr. Spock. It wants terror. Death comes second on its list."

The elevator stopped at the bridge deck, but there was another struggle with its touch plate to get its door open. Nor did they find much cause for cheer as they hurried out of it into the bridge. Sulu, already gasping for breath, was with the technician at the life support station. "Captain, the override is jammed!"

Spock ran to the station. Ripping off a panel, he exposed its mechanism, and kneeling, went to work on it. He was reaching for a tool when Hengist's voice screamed from the bridge speaker. "You are all about to die! Captain Kirk, you are wasting your time!" The voice broke again into its hideous laughter.

"Turn that off, Communications!" Kirk wheeled to Sulu. "Man your post, Mr. Sulu! Prepare all your manual overrides!"

Spock got to his feet. "Normal environmental levels restored, Captain. But, as you know, they won't last long. Several hours with luck."

Sulu asked, "What's going on, Captain?"

"Man your post, Mr. Sulu!" Kirk, aware of his tension, hastened to meet the nurse who was stepping out of the elevator, air hypo in hand. "Is that the tranquilizer?"

"Yes, sir."

"Everyone, including yourself."

The Communications technician had bared his arm for the shot when Hengist's voice spoke once more.

"You cannot stop me now, Captain!" Kirk reached over the crewman's shoulder to push buttons, but the voice wasn't hushed. "Fool, you cannot silence me! I control all the circuits of this ship! You cannot reach me! Your manual overrides' life is as limited as your own. Soon all controls will be mine!"

Kirk moved over to Spock at his computer station. He said softly, "Well, Mr. Spock?"

"Work proceeding, Captain."

This time Kirk raised his voice. "Destroy us—and you destroy yourself."

Chuckles bubbled from the bridge speaker. "I am deathless. I have existed from the dawn of time—and I shall live beyond its end. In the meantime I shall feed—and this time I need no knife. In pain unspeakable you will all die!"

Spock looked up from his work. "It is preparing its feast on terror."

"Imbeciles! I can cut off your oxygen and suffocate you! I can crush you all by increasing atmospheric pressure! I can heighten the temperature till the blood boils in your veins!"

Sulu had received his shot. He turned to Kirk. "Captain," he said cheerfully, "whoever that is, he sure talks gloomy."

"Yes. Stay at your post, Mr. Sulu. If any more systems go out, switch to manual override. Above all, don't be afraid."

"With an arm full of this stuff, sir, I wouldn't be scared of a supernova."

"Ready, Captain," Spock said.

"Implement."

Spock addressed his library computer. "This is a compulsory Class 1 direction. Compute to the last digit the value of pi."

Sharp clicks mingled with an outbreak of buzzing noises. Spock waited. And what he waited for came. Over the speaker Hengist's voice, alarmed, said, "No—not . . ."

Spock made his reply. "The value of pi is a transcendental number without any resolution. All banks of our computer are now working on it to the exclusion of all else. They will continue to calculate this incalculatable number until we order them to stop."

"Let's get back to the Briefing Room," Kirk said. "The Argelians will probably be the first to panic."

Sulu watched them go to the elevator. Then he said happily to himself, "I wonder what I'm supposed to be afraid of."

In the Briefing Room, the body of Hengist was still slumped in the chair where it had been placed. McCoy was circling the table administering the tranquilizer shots. As Kirk and Spock entered, Scott said, "Well, Captain?"

"I don't think our computers will be inhabited by anything but a bunch of figures for a while."

Spock had gone directly to the computer controls. He tested them. "There's some resistance, Captain, but the directive is succeeding. Bank after bank is turning to the problem."

McCoy paused, his air hypo suspended. "If you drive it out of the computer, Jim, it will have to go somewhere else."

"I doubt if it will move into anyone who's been tranquilized, Bones. How're you coming?"

"Almost finished. Just Jaris and me . . ."

He stopped dead. The lights had dimmed again. And there was that rushing sound of vast wings beating. Very gradually, the lights returned. Spock punched a button on the computer controls.

"The entity has fled, Captain," he said.

Kirk had been pondering McCoy's warning. "But where has it fled? Bones—if the thing entered a tranquilized body, what would happen?"

"It might take up knitting," McCoy said. "But nothing more violent than that."

"And you say everyone has had a shot except you— and Jaris?"

Jaris turned in his chair. "You and Mr. Spock have received no shot, Captain."

Kirk looked at him sharply. "That is true. But I know it is not in me—and I'm willing to take a chance on Mr. Spock. Bones, give yourself a shot."

"I ought to stay clear to keep my wits about me," McCoy protested.

"I gave you an order, Bones!"

McCoy stared at Kirk. Then he shrugged, bared his arm and plunged the hypo into it.

"Prefect," Kirk said, "if you will extend your arm, please . . ."

Jaris exploded into an insane howl. Out of his mouth Hengist's voice screamed, *"No! No!"* Leaping from the table, Jaris flung himself on Kirk. Spock raced over to them. The elderly body of Jaris was infused with unbelievable strength. It had Kirk by the throat. Spock tore it away. It shrieked, "Kill! Kill you all! Suffer, suffer! Die!" Grappling with Jaris's fiercely powerful body, Spock reached for its neck to apply the Vulcan pinch. Jaris crumpled. And once again the lights dimmed—the vast wings flapped.

Kirk regained his feet. Around the table its tranquilized people, some sitting, some standing, were smiling as though the struggle had been staged for their entertainment. Yeoman Tancris, her recording pad dropped to the floor, was regarding Spock with a beautiful admiration. From behind her an arm reached out. It encircled her neck, pulling her backward. Hengist's body had left its chair. It whipped out a knife and laid it against the girl's throat.

"Stand away—or I'll kill her!" it said.

McCoy, thoroughly tranquilized, said mildly, "You'll hurt somebody with that knife," and extended a gentle hand toward the weapon. Hengist took a savage swipe at him. Spock jumped him as Kirk ripped the hypo from McCoy. Spock, closing with the howling madman, managed to tear his sleeve. Kirk rammed the hypo home. Hengist wavered in Spock's grasp. "I'll kill you all," he said quietly. "And you shall suffer and I shall feed—" He collapsed.

Kirk grabbed his shoulders. "The Transporter Room! Quickly!" he shouted to Spock.

The Transporter technician beamed at them happily as they staggered into the room, the heavy body of Hengist between them.

Kirk yelled, "Deep space—widest angle of dispersion—full power—maintain . . ."

The Transporter Chief looked at him reproachfully. "No need to get so excited, Captain. I'll take care of it."

"Spock! Do it! Tranquilizers have their limitations!"

Alone, Kirk placed Hengist on the platform. The benevolent Transporter Chief was moving casually toward the console when Spock pushed him aside and seized the controls.

"Energize!" Kirk shouted.

The motionless figure on the platform broke up into sparkle—and was gone.

Spock, his elbow on the console, leaned his head on his hand. Kirk laid a hand on his shoulder. "Quite an expensive little foray into the fleshpots—our visit to Argelius," he said. But the Transporter Chief's feelings were hurt. "You didn't have to shove me, Mr. Spock. I'd have gotten around to it," he said pleasantly. He looked up as Scott and McCoy, both grinning contentedly, opened the door. "Now there are two officers who know how to take life—easy," he said.

"Jaris will be all right," McCoy announced soothingly.

"What did you do with the thing, Captain?" Scott asked. "Send it back to the planet?"

"No, Scotty. We beamed it out into open space at the widest possible dispersion angle."

"But it can't die!" McCoy said.

"Perhaps not, Doctor," Spock said. "Indeed, its consciousness may survive for some time, but only in the form of billions of particles, separate bits of energy, forever drifting in space—powerless, shapeless and without sustenance. We know it must eat to remain alive."

"And it will never feed again, not in the formless state it's in," Kirk said. "Finally, it will die." He looked at McCoy. "Bones—how long before that tranquilizer wears off?"

"Oh, five or six hours, I guess. I certainly have given everyone a pretty good dose."

"So I notice. Well, Mr. Spock, for the next few hours we'll have the happiest crew in space. But I doubt that we get much work done."

"Sir," Spock said, "since, after all, we came to Argelius to rest, I see no reason why we shouldn't take advantage of it."

"Let's go!" Scott cried enthusiastically.

"Shore leave, Mr. Scott? You and Dr. McCoy have still to sleep off the effects of the last one. But we?" Kirk turned to Spock. "Mr. Spock, want to make the rounds of the Argelian fleshpots with me?"

Spock's eyebrows rose. "Captain," he said stiffly, "I spoke of rest."

"Ah," Kirk said. "So you did. My mistake, Mr. Spock."

FOR THE WORLD IS HOLLOW
AND I HAVE TOUCHED THE SKY

(Rik Vollaerts)

That "Bones" McCoy was a lonely man, Kirk knew. That he'd joined the service after some serious personal tragedy in his life, Kirk suspected. What he hadn't realized was the fierce pride in McCoy that made a virtual fetish of silence about any private pain. So he was startled by his violent reaction to the discovery that Nurse Chapel had exceeded what McCoy called her "professional authority."

Entering Sickbay, Kirk found her close to tears. "You had no business to call Captain Kirk!" McCoy was storming at her. "You're excused! You may go to your quarters!"

She blew her nose. "I'm a nurse first, Doctor—and a crew member of the *Enterprise* second," she said, chin firm under her reddened eyes.

"I said you were excused, Nurse!"

Christine swallowed. The hurt in her face was openly appealing. She blew her nose again, looking at Kirk, while McCoy said gruffly, "Christine, please—for God's sake, stop crying! I'll give the Captain a full report, I promise."

She hurried out, and Kirk said, "Well, that was quite a dramatic little scene."

McCoy squared his shoulders. "I've completed the standard physical examinations of the entire crew."

"Good," Kirk said.

"The crew is fit. I found nothing unusual—with one exception."

"Serious?"

"Terminal."

Kirk, shocked, said, "You're sure?"

"Positive. A rare blood disease. Affects one spaceship crew member in fifty thousand."

"What is it?"

"Xenopolycythemia. There is no cure."

"Who?"

"He has one year to live—at the outside chance. He should be relieved of duty as soon as possible."

Kirk spoke quietly. "Who is it, Bones?"

"The ship's chief medical officer."

There was a pause. Then Kirk said, "You mean yourself?"

McCoy reached for a colored tape cartridge on his desk. He stood at stiff attention as he handed it to Kirk. "That's the full report, sir. You'll want it quickly relayed to Starfleet Command—to arrange my replacement."

Wordless, Kirk just looked at him, too stunned to speak. After a moment, he replaced the cartridge on the desk as though it had bit him. McCoy said, "I'll be most effective on the job in the time left to me if you will keep this to yourself."

Kirk shook his head. "There must be *something* that can be done!"

"There isn't." McCoy's voice was harsh. "I've kept up on all the research. I've told you!"

The anguish on Kirk's face broke him. He sank down in the chair at his desk.

"It's terminal, Jim. Terminal."

Though red alert had been called on the *Enterprise*, Kirk was in his quarters. A "replacement" for Bones. Military language was a peculiar thing. How did one "replace" the experience of a human being—the intimacy, the friendship forged out of a thousand shared dangers? "One year to live—at the outside chance." When you got down to the brass tacks of the human portion, you wished that speech had never been invented. But it had been. Like red alerts. They'd been invented, too. In order to remind you that you were Captain of a starship as well as the longtime comrade of a dying man.

As he stepped from the bridge elevator, Spock silently rose from the command chair to relinquish it to him.

"What is that stuff on the screen, Mr. Spock? Those moving pinpoints? A missile spread?"

"A very archaic type, Captain. Sublight space."

"Aye, and chemically fueled to boot, sir," Scott said.

"Anything on communications, Lieutenant Uhura?"

"Nothing, sir. All bands clear."

"Course of the missiles, Mr. Spock?"

"The *Enterprise* would appear to be their target, Captain."

Prepare phaser banks. Yes. Two of them. He gave the order. "Get a fix, Mr. Chekov, on the missiles' point of origin."

"Aye, Captain."

"Mr. Sulu, fire phasers."

The clutch of missiles exploded in a blinding flash. "Well, that's that," Kirk said. "Mr. Chekov, alter course to missile point of origin."

"Course change laid in, sir."

"Warp three, Mr. Sulu."

Spock spoke from the computer station. "They were very ancient missiles, Captain. Sensor reading indicates an age of over ten thousand years."

"Odd," said Kirk. "How could they still be functional?"

"They evidently had an inertial guidance system that made any other communications control unnecessary."

"And the warheads, Captain," Scott said. "Nuclear fusion type according to my readings."

Spock spoke again. "We're approaching the coordinates of the hostile vessel, Captain."

"Get it on the screen, Mr. Sulu."

The term "vessel" seemed to be inappropriate. What had appeared on the screen was a huge asteroid. It was roughly round, jagged, its rocky mass pitted by thousands of years of meteor hits.

"Mr. Spock, we've got maximum magnification. Is the object on the screen what it looks to be—an asteroid?"

"Yes, sir. Some two hundred miles in diameter."

"Could the hostile vessel be hiding behind it?"

"Impossible, Captain. I've had that area under scanner constantly."

"Then the missiles' point of origin is that asteroid?"

"Yes, sir."

Kirk got up and went to Spock's station "Full sensor probe, Mr. Spock."

After a moment, Spock withdrew his head from his computer's hood. "Typical asteroid chemically but it is not orbiting, Captain. It is pursuing an independent course through this solar system."

"How can it?" Kirk said. "Unless it's powered—a spaceship!"

Spock cocked an eyebrow in what for him was amazement. Then he said slowly, "It *is* under power—and correcting for all gravitational stresses." He dived under his hood again.

"Power source?" Kirk asked.

"Atomic, very archaic. Leaving a trail of debris and hard radiation."

Kirk frowned briefly. "Plot the course of the asteroid, Mr. Chekov."

Once more Spock withdrew his head. "The asteroid's outer shell is hollow. It surrounds an independent inner core with a breathable atmosphere—sensors record no life forms."

"Then it must be on automatic controls," contributed Scott.

Spock nodded. "And its builders—or passengers—are dead."

Chekov said, "Course of asteroid—I mean spaceship—241 mark 17."

Spock had stooped swiftly to his console. He pushed several controls. Then he looked up. "Sir, that reading Ensign Chekov just gave us puts the asteroid ship on a collision course with planet Daran V!"

"Daran V!" Kirk stared at him. "My memory banks say that's an inhabited planet, Mr. Spock!"

"Yes, sir. Population, approximately three billion, seven hundred and twenty-four million." He paused, glancing back at his console panel. "Estimated time of impact: thirteen months, six days."

"Well," Kirk said. "That's a pretty extensive population." He whirled to Sulu. "Mr. Sulu, match *Enterprise* speed with the asteroid ship's. Mr. Spock and I are transporting aboard her. Mr. Scott, you have the con."

They entered the Transporter Room to see Christine Chapel handing his tricorder to McCoy. "A lot can happen in a year," she was saying. "Give yourself every minute of it."

"Thanks," McCoy said, and slung the tricorder over his shoulder. Ignoring Kirk and Spock, he stepped up on the Transporter platform, taking position on one of its circles.

Kirk walked over to him. "Bones," he said, "Spock and I will handle this one."

"Without me?" McCoy said. "You'll never make it back here without me."

"I feel it would be wiser if . . ."

"I'm fine, thank you, Captain," McCoy brushed him off. "I want to go."

So that was how Bones wanted it played. He wasn't fatally ill. The word terminal might never have been spoken. "All right, Bones. You're probably right. If we make it back here, we'll need you with us." He took up his own position on the platform between Spock and McCoy.

They arrived on a land area of the asteroid ship. As though land on an asteroid weren't strange enough, strange plants, coiling black tendrils abounded, their strange roots sunk in deep, smoking fissures. High mountains shouldered up in the distance. Otherwise, the view showed only rubble and pockmarked rocks.

McCoy said, "You'd swear you were on a planet's surface."

Spock tossed away a stone he'd examined. "The question is, why make a ship look like a planet?"

"You wouldn't even know you were on a spaceship." Kirk jerked his com unit from his belt. "Kirk to *Enterprise*."

"Scott here, Captain."

"Transported without incident. Kirk out." He rehung his communicator on his belt, and was moving forward when, to his far left, his eye caught the glint of sunlight on metal. "Over there," he said. "Look . . ."

It was a row of metal cylinders. They were all about

eight feet high, their width almost matching their height, and regularly spaced fifty feet apart. The men approached the nearest one, examining it carefully without touching it. "No apparent opening," Kirk observed.

"Spock, you found no intelligent life forms," McCoy said, "but surely these are evidence of . . ."

"This asteroid ship is ten thousand years old, Doctor. They may be evidence of the existence of some previous life forms." He checked his tricorder. "Certainly, there are no signs of life now."

They eyed the enigmatic cylinder again before they walked on to the next one. It was a duplicate of the first. As they reached the third, the two cylinders behind them suddenly opened, disgorging two groups of men, clad in shaggy homespun. Armed with short daggers and broadswords, they moved silently, trailing the *Enterprise* trio. A slim and beautiful woman followed them. She halted as the men charged.

The struggle was quick and violent. Outnumbered, Spock took several blows from sword hilts before he dropped to the ground, half-conscious. McCoy, head down, rushed a man off his feet, the momentum of his plunge crashing him into the woman. Her eyes widened in a surprise that contained no fear. Startled by her beauty, McCoy was brought up short, taking in the lustrous black hair piled on her head in fantastic loops, her glittering black leotardlike garment. Then he was stunned by a smash on the head. Kirk, going down under a swarming attack, saw the broadsword lifting up over McCoy and yelled, *"Bones!"*

The woman raised her right hand.

The broadsword was stayed in midstroke. McCoy was pulled to his feet. He shook his head, trying to clear it. Vaguely, he became aware of hands fumbling at his belt. Then his arms were jerked behind his back. Disarmed of phasers and communicators, he, Kirk and Spock were herded over to the woman.

"These are your weapons?" she asked, holding their belts in her right hand.

"Yes," Kirk said. "Of a kind. Weapons and communication devices. Let me help my friend!" He struggled to pull free. The woman made a commanding gesture.

Released, he rushed over to the still groggy McCoy. "Bones, are you all right?"

"I—I think so, Jim."

The woman's dark eyes were on McCoy. "I am called Natira," she told him. "I am the High Priestess of the People. Welcome to the world of Yonada."

"We have received more desirable welcomes," Kirk said.

She ignored him. "Bring them!" she ordered their guards.

She led the way to an open cylinder. They were in an apparently endless, lighted corridor, lined by curious people in their homespun clothing. As Natira passed them, they bowed deeply. She was nearing an arched portal. It was flanked by two ornately decorated pillars, their carvings suggestive of a form of writing, cut deep into the stone. Natira, bowing herself, touched some hidden device that opened the massive door. But keen-eyed Spock had registered its location. He had also observed the writing.

The large room they entered was dim, its sole light a glow that shone from under its central dais. Its rich ornamentation matched that of the portal.

"You will kneel," Natira said.

There was no point, Kirk thought, in making an issue of it. He nodded at Spock and McCoy. They knelt. Natira, stepping onto the dais, turned to what was clearly an altar. Etched into its stone was a design that resembled a solar system. As Natira fell to her knees before the altar, light filled the room.

McCoy, his voice lowered, said, "She called this the world. These people don't know they're on a spaceship."

Kirk nodded. "Possible. The ship's been in flight for a long time."

"That writing," Spock said, "resembles the lexicography of the Fabrini."

But Natira, her arms upraised, was speaking. "O Oracle of the People, O most wise and most perfect, strangers have come to our world. They bear instruments we do not understand."

Light blazed from the altar. As though it had

strengthened her to ask the question, she rose to her feet, turned and said, "Who are you?"

"I am Captain Kirk of the Starship *Enterprise*. This is Dr. McCoy, our Medical Officer. Mr. Spock is my First Officer."

"And for what reason do you visit this world?"

The word "world" again. Kirk and McCoy exchanged a look.

"We come in friendship," Kirk said.

The sound of thunder crashed from the altar. A booming echo of the thunder, the voice of the Oracle spoke.

"Learn what it means to be our enemy. Learn what that means before you learn what it means to be our friend."

Lightning flashed. The three *Enterprise* men were felled to the floor by a near-lethal charge of electricity.

McCoy was taking too long to recover consciousness. He continued to lay, white-faced, in a sleeping alcove of their lavishly decorated guest quarters. Spock, who had been trying to work out muscle spasms in his shoulders, joined Kirk at McCoy's couch.

"He must have suffered an excessively intense electrical shock," he said.

"No. I don't think that's it," Kirk said. He reached for McCoy's pulse. Spock, aware of the deep concern in Kirk's face, was puzzled. "Nothing else could have caused this, sir." He paused. "That is—nothing that has occurred down *here*."

Kirk glanced up at Spock. He knew that the Vulcan had sensed something of the real cause of his anxiety. "The shock was unusually serious because of McCoy's weakened condition," he said.

"May I ask precisely what is troubling the Doctor?"

"Yes, Mr. Spock. He'd never tell you himself. But now I think he'd want you to know. He has xenopolycythemia."

Spock stiffened. After a long moment, he said quietly, "I know of the disease, Captain."

"Then you know there's nothing that can be done." As he spoke, McCoy stirred. His eyes opened. Kirk stooped over him. "How is it now, Bones?"

"All right," McCoy said. He sat up, pulling himself rapidly together. "How are *you*, Spock?"

"Fine, thank you. The Captain and I must have received a less violent electrical charge."

Falsely hearty, McCoy said, "That Oracle really got to me. I must be especially susceptible to his magic spells."

"Spock knows," Kirk said. "I told him, Bones."

There was relief in McCoy's face. He stood up. "Hadn't we better find this ship's control room and get these people off their collision course?"

"You're in no shape to be up," Kirk said.

"Ridiculous!" McCoy said. *"I'm up!"*

Kirk saw one of the alcove's curtains sway. He strode to it, jerking it aside. A shabby old man, fear in his face, was huddled against the wall. He peered into Kirk's face. What he saw in it must have reassured him. He moved away from the wall, hesitated, took some powder from a pouch hung over his shoulder. "For strength," he said. He held out the pouch to them. "Many of us have felt the power of our Oracle. This powder will be of benefit. You are not of Yonada."

"No," Kirk said gently. "We come from outside your world."

The old hand reached out to touch Kirk's arm. "You are as we are?"

"The same," Kirk said.

"You are the first to come here. I am ignorant. Tell me of the outside."

"What do you wish to know?"

"Where is outside?"

Kirk pointed skyward. "It's up there."

The filmed eyes glanced up at the ceiling. Like a child put off by an adult lie, the old man looked back at Kirk in mixed disbelief and disappointment. Kirk smiled at him. "The outside is up there and all around."

"So *they* say, also," the old man said sadly. "Years ago, I climbed the mountains, even though it is forbidden."

"Why is it forbidden?" Kirk asked.

"I am not sure. But things are not as they teach us— for the world is hollow and I have touched the sky."

The voice had sunk into a terrified whisper. As he

uttered the last words, the old man screamed in sudden agony, clutching at his temples. He collapsed in a sprawl-ed heap on the floor. Horrified, Kirk saw a spot on one temple flash into a pulsating glow. Then the flare died.

McCoy examined the spot. "Something under the skin." He moved the shabby homespun to check the heart. "Jim, he's dead."

Kirk looked down at the heap. " 'For the world is hollow and I have touched the sky.' What an epitaph for a human life!"

Spock said, "He said it was forbidden to climb the mountains."

"Of course it's forbidden," Kirk said. "If you climbed the mountains, you might discover you were living in an asteroid spaceship, not in the world at all. *That* I'll bet is the forbidden knowledge."

"What happened?"

It was Natira. She had entered their quarters with two women bearing platters of fruit and wine. At the sight of the crumpled body, their faces convulsed with terror. But Natira knelt down beside it.

"We don't know what happened," Kirk told her. "He suddenly screamed in pain—and died."

She bent her head in prayer. "Forgive him, O Oracle, most wise and most perfect. He was an old man—and old men are sometimes foolish." She rose to her feet. "But it is written that those of the People who sin or speak evil will be punished."

The severity in her face softened into sadness. She touched a wall button. To the guards who entered she said, "Take him away—gently. He served well and for many years." Then she spoke to the women. "Place the food on the table and go."

As the door closed behind them, she crossed to McCoy. "You do not seem well. It is distressing to me."

"No," he said. "I am all right."

"It is the wish of the Oracle that you now be treated as honored guests. I will serve you with my own hands." But the tray she arranged with fruit and wine was taken to McCoy. When she left them to prepare the other trays, Kirk said, "You seem favored, Bones."

"Indeed, Doctor," Spock said, "the lady has shown a preference for you from the beginning."

"Nobody can blame her for that," McCoy retorted.

"Personally," Kirk said, "I find her taste questionable." McCoy, sipping wine, said, "My charm has always been fatal," but Kirk noted that his eyes were nevertheless fixed on the graceful bend of the woman at the table. "If it's so fatal," he said, "why don't you arrange to spend some time alone with the lady? Then Spock and I might find a chance to locate the power controls of this place."

Natira was back, holding two goblets of wine. "It is time that our other guests refresh themselves."

Kirk lifted his goblet. "To our good friends of Yonada."

"We are most interested in your world," Spock said.

"That pleases us."

"Then perhaps you wouldn't mind if we looked around a bit," Kirk ventured.

"You will be safe," she said. "The People know of you now."

McCoy coughed uncomfortably. She went to him swiftly. "I do not think you are yet strong enough to look around with your friends."

"Perhaps not," he smiled.

"Then why not remain here? Rest—and we will talk." She *was* beautiful. "I should like that," McCoy said.

She turned to Kirk. "But you—you and Mr. Spock— you are free to go about and meet our People."

"Thank you," he said. "We appreciate your looking after Dr. McCoy."

"Not at all," she inclined her head. "We shall make him well." She saw them to the door. Then she hastened back to McCoy. As she sat down on the couch beside him, he said, "I am curious. How did the Oracle punish the old man?"

The dark lashes lowered. "I—cannot tell you now."

"There's some way by which the Oracle knows what you say, isn't there?"

"What we say—what we think. The Oracle knows the minds and hearts of all the People."

McCoy's forehead creased with a worried frown.

Concerned, Natira extended a white hand that tried to stroke the frown away. "I did not know you would be hurt so badly."

"Perhaps we had to learn the power of the Oracle."

"McCoy. There is something I must say. Since the moment I saw you—" She took a deep breath. "It is not the custom of the People to hide their feelings."

McCoy said to himself, Watch your step, boy. But to her, he said, "Honesty is usually wisdom."

"Is there a woman for you?" she asked.

He could smell the fragrance of the lustrous black hair near his shoulder. This woman was truthful as well as beautiful. So he gave her the truth. "No," he said. "No, there isn't."

The lashes lifted—and he got the full impact of her open femininity. "Does McCoy find me attractive?"

"Yes," he said. "I do. I do indeed."

She took his face between her hands, looking deep into his eyes. "I hope you men of space—of other worlds, hold truth as dear as we do."

Watching his step was becoming difficult. "We do," he said.

"It is dear to me," she said. "So I wish you to stay here on Yonada. I want you for my mate."

McCoy took one of the hands from his face and kissed it. The Eagle Scout in him whispered, Brother, douse this campfire. But in him was also a man under sentence of death; a man with one year to live—one with a new, very intense desire to make that last year count. He turned the hand over to kiss its palm. "But we are strangers to each other," he said.

"Is it not the nature of men and women—that pleasure lies in learning about each other?"

"Yes."

"Then let the thought rest in your heart, McCoy, while I tell you about the Promise. In the fullness of time, the People will reach a new world, rich, green, so lovely to the eyes it will fill them with tears of joy. You can share that new world with me. You shall be its master because you'll be my master."

"When will you reach this new world?"

"Soon. The Oracle will only say—soon."

There was an innocence about her that opened his heart. Incredibly, he heard himself cry out, "Natira, Natira, if you only knew how much I've needed a future!"

"You have been lonely," she said. She picked up the wine glass and held it to his lips. "It is all over, the loneliness. There shall be no more loneliness for you."

He drank and set the glass aside. "Natira—there's something I must tell you . . ."

"Sssh," she said. "There is nothing you need to say."

"But there is."

She removed the hand she had placed over his mouth. "Then tell me, if the telling is such a need."

"I am ill," he said. "I have an illness for which there is no cure. I have one year to live, Natira."

The dark eyes did not flinch. "A year can be a lifetime, McCoy."

"It is my entire lifetime."

"Until I saw you my heart was empty. It sustained my life—and nothing more. Now it sings. I am grateful for the feeling that you have made it feel whether it lasts for a day—a month—a year—whatever time the Creators give to us."

He took her in his arms.

Kirk and Spock were meeting curious looks as they walked down a corridor of the asteroid ship. The more people they encountered, the clearer it became they had no inkling of the real nature of their world. Spock said, "Whoever built this ship must have given them a religion that would control their curiosity."

"Judging by the old man, suppressing curiosity is handled very directly," Kirk said. They had reached the portal of the Oracle Room. Pretending to a casual interest in its carved stone pillars, Spock eyed them keenly. "Yes," he said, "the writing is that of the Fabrini. I can read it."

"Fabrina?" Kirk said. "Didn't the sun of the Fabrina system go nova and destroy its planets?"

"It did, Captain. Toward the end, the Fabrini lived underground as the people do here."

"Perhaps some of them were put aboard this ship to be sent to another planet." Kirk glanced up and down the corridor. It was almost empty. "And these are their descendants."

They were alone now in the corridor. Kirk tried and failed to open the Oracle Room's door. Spock touched the secret opening device set into one of the pillars. Inside, they flattened themselves against a wall. The door closed behind them. Nothing happened. Kirk, his voice low, said, "The Oracle doesn't seem to know we are here. What alerted it the first time?"

Spock moved a few steps toward the central dais. "Captain, the Oracle's misbehavior occurred when Natira knelt on that platform." Kirk stepped onto the platform. He walked carefully around it. Again, nothing happened. "Mr. Spock, continue investigating. The clue to the control place must be here somewhere." But carvings on a wall had caught Spock's attention. "More writing," he said. "It says nothing to suggest this is anything but a planet. Nor is there any question that the builders of the ship are to be considered gods."

Kirk had found a stone monolith set in a niche. It bore a carved design of a sun and planets. Spock joined him. "Eight planets, Captain. Eight. That was the number in the solar system of Fabrina."

"Then there's no doubt that these People are the Fabrini's descendants?"

"None, sir. And no doubt they have been in flight on this asteroid ship for ten thousand years." As Spock spoke, there was the sound of the door opening. They hastily slid behind the monolith. Kirk cautiously peered around it to see Natira, alone, crossing the room to the platform. She knelt. As before, hot light flared from the altar.

"Speak," said the Oracle.

"It is I, Natira."

"Speak."

"It is written that only the High Priestess of the People may select her mate."

"It is so written."

"For the rest of the People—mating and bearing is only permitted by the will of the Creators."

"Of necessity. Our world is small."

"The three strangers among us—there is one among

them called McCoy. I wish him to remain with the People—as my mate."

Kirk gave a soundless whistle. Bones certainly had lost no time. Spock cocked an eyebrow, looking at Kirk.

"Does the stranger agree to this?" queried the Oracle.

"I have asked him. He has not yet given me his answer."

"He must become one of the People. He must worship the Creators and agree to the insertion of the obedience instrument."

"He will be told what must be done."

"If he agrees to all things, it is permitted. Teach him our laws so that he commits no sacrilege, no offense against the People—or the Creators."

"It shall be as you say, O most wise."

Natira rose, bowed twice, backed away from the altar and walked toward the door. As Kirk watched her go, his sleeve brushed against the monolith's carved design. The Oracle Room reverberated with a high-pitched, ululating whine. Natira wheeled from the door. The whine turned to a blazing white light. It turned to focus on Kirk and Spock. They went rigid, unable to move.

Natira rushed to the altar.

"Who are the intruders?" demanded the booming voice.

"Two of the strangers."

"McCoy is one of them?"

"No."

"These two have committed sacrilege. You know what must be done."

"I know."

Guards rushed into the room. The light that held Kirk and Spock died, leaving them dazed. Natira pointed to them. "Take them," she told the guards.

As they were seized, she walked up to them. "You have been most foolish," she said. "You have misused our hospitality. And you have more seriously sinned—a sin for which death is the punishment!"

Natira withstood the storm of McCoy's wrath quietly. As he paused in his furious pacing of her quarters, she said—and for the third time—"They entered the Oracle Room."

"And why is death the penalty for that?" he shouted. "They acted out of ignorance!"

"They said they came in friendship. They betrayed our trust. I can make no other decision."

He wheeled to face her. "Natira, you must let them return to their ship!"

"I cannot."

"For me," he said. He pulled her from her couch and into his arms. "I have made my decision. I'm staying with you—here on Yonada."

She swayed with the relief of her love. Into the ear against his cheek, McCoy said, "What they did, they did because they thought they had to. You will not regret letting them go. I am happy for the first time in my life. How can I remain happy, knowing you commanded the death of my friends?"

She lifted her mouth for his kiss. "So be it," she said. "I will give you their lives to show you my love."

"My heart sings now," McCoy said. "Let me tell them. They will need their communications units to return to their ship."

"Very well, McCoy. All shall be as you wish."

He left her for the corridor where Kirk and Spock were waiting under guard. He nodded to the guards. When they disappeared down the corridor, he handed the communicators to Kirk. Kirk passed one to Spock. "Where's yours?" he asked. "You're coming with us, aren't you?"

"No, I'm not," McCoy said.

"But this isn't a planet, Bones! It's a spaceship on a collision course with Daran V!"

"Jim, I'm on something of a collision course myself."

"I order you to return to the ship, Dr. McCoy!"

"And I refuse! I intend to stay right here—on this ship. Natira has asked me to stay. So I shall stay."

"As her husband?"

"Yes. I love her." There were tears in his eyes. "Is it so much to ask, Jim, to let me love?"

"No." Kirk straightened his shoulders. "But does she know—how much of a future you'll have together?"

"Yes. I have told her."

"Bones, if the course of this ship isn't corrected, we'll have to blow it out of space."

"I'll find a way—or you will. You won't destroy Yonada and the people."

Kirk shook his head. "This isn't like you—suddenly giving up—quitting—not fighting any more. You're sick—and you're hiding behind a woman's skirts!"

McCoy swung a fist and Kirk took it square on the chin. He staggered. Spock steadied him. McCoy was yelling, "Sick? Not fighting? Come on, Captain! Try me again!"

Very grave, Spock said, "This conduct is very unlike you, Doctor."

Kirk fumbled for his communicator. "Kirk calling *Enterprise*. Come in, *Enterprise*."

"Scott here, Captain."

"Lock in on our signals. Transport Mr. Spock and me aboard at once."

"What about Dr. McCoy?"

Yes, indeed. What *about* Doctor McCoy? He looked at his friend. "He is staying here, Mr. Scott. Kirk out."

Spock moved to Kirk, flipping open his own communicator. McCoy backed away. They broke into sparkle—and were gone. Savagely, McCoy dragged a sleeve over his tear-blinded eyes.

Custom required him to stand alone before the Oracle.

It spoke.

"To become one of the People of Yonada, the instrument of obedience must be made part of your flesh. Do you now give your consent?"

Natira came forward. She crossed to another side of the altar and opened a small casket.

"I give my consent," McCoy said. As she removed a small device from the casket, her dark eyes met his with a look of pure love. "Say now, McCoy," she said. "For once it is done, it is done."

"Let it be done," he said.

She came to him. Placing the device against his temple, she activated it. He heard a hissing sound.

There was a thudding in his head. Instinctively his hand went to the place of insertion. "You are now one with my People," she said. "Kneel with me."

He reached for her hand. She said, "I here pledge you the love you want and will make beautiful your time."

"We are now of one mind," he said.

"One heart."

"One life," he said.

"We shall build the new world of the Promise together, O most wise and most perfect." They rose. She moved into his arms and he kissed her.

The Oracle said, "Teach him what he must know as one of the people."

Natira bowed. Obediently, she led McCoy to the stone monolith. She touched a button—and the carved inset depicting a sun and eight planets slid aside to reveal a large book. "This is the Book of the People," she said. "It is to be opened and read when we reach the world of the Promise. It was given by the Creators."

"Do the People know the contents of the book?"

"Only that it tells of our world here. And why we must one day leave it for the new one."

"Has the reason for leaving been revealed to the People?"

"No! It has not."

Then they'd been right, McCoy realized. Yonada's inhabitants were unaware they lived on a spaceship. "Has it been revealed to you, Natira? As the Priestess of the People?"

She shook her head. "I know only of the new world promised to us, much greater than this little one— verdant and fruitful but empty of living beings. It waits for us."

"Don't you long to know the book's secrets?"

"It is enough for me to know that we shall understand all that now is hidden when we reach our home." She touched the button in the monolith. Its carved inset slid back.

"What is the law concerning the book?"

"To touch it—to allow it to be seen by a nonbeliever is blasphemy to be punished by death."

On the *Enterprise* Kirk had made his first act a report to Starfleet Command. It had to be told, not only of McCoy's critical illness, but of their failure to correct the collision course of the asteroid ship. Its Chief of Operations, Admiral Westervliet himself, appeared on the screen in Kirk's quarters to respond to the news.

"Medical Headquarters will supply you with a list of space physicians and their biographies, Captain. You will find a replacement for Dr. McCoy among them."

Kirk addressed the stiffly mustached face on the screen. "Yes, Admiral. However, Starfleet's orders to continue our mission is creating difficulties."

"Difficulties? Perhaps I've failed to make myself clear, Captain. You have been relieved of all responsibility for alteration of the course of the asteroid ship Yonada. Starfleet Command will take care of the situation."

"That is the problem, sir," Kirk said.

"A problem? For whom?"

"My crew, sir. Dr. McCoy's illness has become generally known. His condition forced us to leave him on Yonada. His safety depends on the safety of Yonada. To leave this area before Yonada's safety is certain would create a morale problem for the crew. It's a purely human one, of course."

Westervliet had a habit of attacking his mustache when human problems were mentioned. Now it was taking a beating.

"Yes," he said. "Well, Captain Kirk, I certainly sympathize with your wish to remain in Dr. McCoy's vicinity. But the general mission of the *Enterprise* is galactic investigation. You will continue with it."

"Yes, Admiral," Kirk said. "One request, however. Should a cure for Doctor McCoy's disease be discovered, will you advise the *Enterprise?*"

"That is not a request, Captain. Between you and me, it's an order, isn't it?"

"Yes, sir. Thank you, sir."

Kirk, switching off the screen, sat still in his chair.

McCoy had made his choice. No appeal had been able to change it. And who was to say it wasn't the right one? A year of life with a woman's love against a year of life without it. Bones. He was going to miss him. The intercom squeaked. He rose to hit the button. "Kirk here."

"Dr. McCoy for you, Captain," Uhura said. "He has an urgent message."

"Put him on!"

"Jim?"

"Yes, Bones."

"We may be able to get these people back on course!"

Kirk's pulse raced. "Have you located the controls?"

"No—but I've seen a book that contains all the knowledge of Yonada's builders. If you can get to it, Spock can dig out the information."

"Where is it?" Kirk asked.

A scream of agony burst from the intercom. "Bones! What's happening? Bones!"

Silence. Frantic, Kirk tried again. "McCoy, what *is* it? What has been done to you? Bones, come in . . ."

But he knew what had happened. Torture, death.

The Oracle had taken McCoy's life in exchange for his forbidden revelation.

Kirk's jaw muscles set hard. "Transporter Room," he told the intercom.

He and Spock materialized in Natira's quarters. She was cradling McCoy's head in her arms. But his face was contorted with pain. Kirk saw him struggle to lift his head. It sank back into Natira's lap.

She looked at them. Dully, her voice toneless, she said, "You have killed your friend. I will have you put to death."

"Let me help you," Kirk said.

"Until you are dead, he will think of you and disobey. While you live, my beloved cannot forget you. So I shall see you die."

She made a move to get up and Kirk grabbed her, clapping his hand over her mouth. "Spock," he said, "help McCoy."

"Yes, Captain." Spock unslung his tricorder. From it he removed a tiny electronic device. Bending over McCoy's motionless body, he pressed the device on the spot where the instrument of obedience had been inserted. When he withdrew it, the insert was clinging to it. He jerked it clear. Then he handed it to Natira. She stared at him, unbelieving. A little moan broke from her. Kirk released her. She sank to the floor. After a moment, she pulled herself up to her hands and knees and crawled over to McCoy. She touched his temple. "My beloved is again a stranger. We are no longer one life." She burst into passionate weeping. "Why have you done this to us? Why?"

"He is still yours," Kirk said gently.

The tears choked her. "It is—forbidden. He is not of our people—now. You have released him—from his vow of obedience."

"We have released him from the cruelty of your Oracle," Kirk said.

She closed her eyes, unhearing, her body racked with sobs. Beside her, Kirk saw McCoy's eyelids flicker open. He went to him quickly, bending over him. "You spoke of a book," he said. "Where is it, Bones?"

Natira leaped to her feet with a shriek. "You must not know! You must not know that!"

McCoy looked up into Kirk's eyes. "The Oracle Room," he whispered.

"You will never see the Book!" cried Natira. "It is blasphemy!" She ran to the door, calling, "Guards! Guards!"

Kirk caught her, closing his hand over her mouth again. "You must listen to me, Natira!" She pulled away from him and he jerked her back. *"Listen to me! If you do not understand what I tell you, you may call the guards. And we will accept whatever punishment is decreed. But now you must listen!"*

She slowly lifted the tear-wet lashes. "What is it you wish to say?"

"I shall tell you the truth, Natira—the truth about your world of Yonada. And you will trust it as true as a child trusts what is true. Years ago, ten thousand years ago, a sun died and the sun's worlds died with it.

Its worlds were the eight ones you see pictured on the stone pillar in the Oracle Room."

"Yonada is one of those worlds," she said.

"No. It was the world of your ancestors—your creators." He paused to give her time. After a moment, he quietly added, "It no longer exists, Natira."

"You are mad," she whispered. "You are mad."

"Hear me out, Natira! Your ancestors knew their world was about to die. They wanted their race to live. So they built a great ship. On it they placed their best people. Then they sent them and the ship into space."

"You wish me to believe that Yonada is a ship?"

"Yes," Kirk said.

"But we have a sun! It did not die. And at night I see the stars!"

"No. You have never seen the sun. You have never seen the stars. You live inside a hollow ball. Your fathers created the ball to protect you—to take you on the great journey to the new safe world of the Promise."

In her face he could see half-thought thoughts reviving, completing themselves. But the growing perception was painful. Yet it had come. She spoke very slowly. "The truth—why do you bring it to Yonada?"

"We had to. Your ship has done well—but its machinery is tired. It must be mended. If we don't mend it, Yonada will strike and kill another great world it knows nothing about."

Belief flooded into her. With it came the realization of betrayal.

"Why has this truth not been told us? Why have we been kept in darkness?"

Kirk went to her. But she pushed him away, overwhelmed by the sense of an incredible treachery. "No! You have lied! I believe only the Oracle! I must believe!"

Kirk said, "Let us remove the instrument of obedience. Let us remove it for the truth's sake."

She was gone, fled out the door. Kirk turned to Spock. "Do you think she understood me?" he said. But Spock was at the open door. Kirk saw him nod pleasantly to a passing guard before he quietly closed the door. "She hasn't sent the guards to detain us, Captain. It is my supposition that she understood a great deal."

Behind them, McCoy had struggled shakily to his feet. Now he pushed past them. "Natira! I have to go to her. I must go to her in the Oracle Room."

She was on her knees before the altar, her eyes shut in rapt devotion.

The thunder voice spoke. "You have listened to the words of the nonbelievers."

"I have listened."

"You felt the pain of warning."

"I felt the pain of warning."

"Why did you listen further?"

"They said they spoke the truth."

"Their truth is not your truth."

She opened her eyes. "Is truth not truth for all?"

"There is only one for you. Repent your disobedience."

"I must know the truth of the world!" she cried.

At the sound of her scream, Kirk rushed into the Oracle Room. He lifted Natira from the dais, but McCoy, reaching for her, took her in his arms, holding her close. Her body was stiff under spasms of pain. As one passed, she reached out a hand to caress his face. "Your friends have told me—much."

"They spoke the truth," McCoy said.

"I believe you. I believe . . ."

Agony convulsed her again. She fought it bravely. "I believe with you, my husband. We have been kept in darkness."

McCoy extended a hand to Spock. The tiny electronic device performed its function once more. When McCoy lifted it from Natira's temple, it held the obedience insert. He held it up for her to see. The grief of a great loss shadowed her dark eyes as she lapsed into unconsciousness.

"Is she all right?" Kirk asked.

"She will be. I'll stay with her."

Kirk said, "Mr. Spock—the Fabrina inset."

They were crossing to the monolith when the Oracle

spoke, a fierce anger in its voice. "You blaspheme the temple!"

Kirk turned. "We do this for the survival of Yonada's people."

"You are forbidden to gaze at the Book!"

"We must consult it to help the people!"

"The punishment is death."

Kirk looked back at McCoy. "Bones?"

"Depress the side section," McCoy said.

A blast of heat struck them. Around them the walls had turned a radiant red. Even as he pressed the side of the monolith, the air he breathed was scorching Kirk's lungs. But the inset had slid open. He seized the book and passed it to Spock. "It must contain the plan. Is it indexed?"

"Yes, Captain. Here's the page . . ."

Yellow, brittle with age, the page's parchment showed the same idealized sun, the same planet placements as the altar design and the inset. Arrows pointed to three of the planets. Spock translated the Fabrini writing at the top of the page. "Apply pressure simultaneously to the planets indicated."

The walls were glowing hotter. Spock tossed the book aside and they raced for the altar plaque. As Kirk pushed at the three planets, the altar moved forward. Then it stopped. Spock slid into the space behind it. Before he followed him, Kirk turned back to McCoy and Natira. "Let's get out of this heat," he called.

Spock had found a short passageway. As he approached its end wall, it lifted. At once he heard the hum of electronic power. A light shone on a button-crowded console. Spock studied it for a moment. Then he pressed a button. The light went out. "I've neutralized that heating element!" he called back to the others.

The heat in the Oracle Room rapidly cooled. Kirk and McCoy sat Natira down against an altar wall. "You'll be all right here now," Kirk said. "The Oracle can no longer punish."

He saw her rest her glossy head against McCoy's shoulder. Looking up at him, she said, "Your friends have ended the punishments?" He nodded. "And will they send this—this ship on to the place of the Promise?"

"Yes," he said. "That is their promise. Now I must help them. Come with me."

"No," she said.

"There is nothing to fear now, Natira. So come. We must hurry to join them."

"No. I cannot go with you." She paused. "It is not fear that holds me. I now understand the great purpose of our fathers. I must honor it, McCoy."

He stared at her in unbelief. "You mean to stay here—on Yonada?"

"I must remain with my people throughout our great journey."

"Natira, trust me! The Oracle will not harm us!"

"I stay because it is what I must do," she said.

"I will not leave you," McCoy said.

"Will McCoy stay here to die?"

The question shocked him into silence. He fell to his knees beside her. "Natira, you have given me reason to wish to live. But wishing is not enough. I must search through the universe to cure myself—and all those like me. I wanted you with me—with me . . ."

"This is my universe," she said. "You came here to save my people. Shall I abandon them?"

"I love you," McCoy said.

She kissed him. "If it is permitted, perhaps one day you, too, will see the land of our Promise. . . ."

It was good-bye. And he knew it. He reached for her blindly through a mist of tears.

In the asteroid ship's control room, Spock had located a weakness in one of its consoles' eight tubes.

"Enough to turn it off course?" Kirk asked.

"Yes, Captain. The engine can take a check." Kirk, studying control panels, was reminded of those of the *Enterprise*. "A very simple problem," Spock called from the engine room. "And comparatively easy to repair."

He came back, holding one hand out stiffly. "I think we can now attempt the course correction, sir."

"What was wrong?"

"In creating a completely natural environment for the people on this ship, its builders included many life forms—including insects. A control jet in thore was blocked by a hornets' nest."

"You're not serious, Mr. Spock?"

Spock held up a forefinger. It was swollen to twice its normal size. "I destroyed the nest," he said. "In doing so, I was stung." He sat down, resuming his watch of the console instruments. "The guidance system is taking over, sir. I think we can revert to automatic controls."

"She's steady on course now," Kirk said.

They released the manual controls and were heading back to the Oracle Room when Spock stopped at a screened console of complex design. "Knowledge files," he said. "Those banks are filled with the total knowledge of the Fabrini. I presume they were prepared for the people to consult when they reach their destination." He left Kirk to examine the console more closely. "They seem to have amassed a great deal of medical knowledge."

Unslinging his tricorder, he slipped a taped disk into it. He passed it over the console. "The knowledge of the builders of this ship could be extremely valuable— even though it is ten thousand years old."

McCoy spoke from behind them. "Gentlemen, are we ready to return to the *Enterprise?*"

Kirk stared at him. It was best to ask no questions, he thought. "Yes, Bones, we are," he said. He flipped open his com unit. "Kirk to *Enterprise*. Landing party ready to beam aboard."

The screen in Sickbay held a series of chemical formulas in the Fabrini writing. Kirk and Spock, watching Christine Chapel prepare another air-hypo injection, saw that her hands were shaking. She noticed it, too. To quiet her agitation, she glanced at the life indicators at the head of McCoy's bed. The steady blinking of their lights steadied her. She thrust the air-hypo into a green liquid.

"Not another one?" McCoy said as she approached his bed. He made a face as the hypo took effect. But already it had made a fast change in the life support panel.

"Excellent, Doctor," Christine said. "You're quite able to see for yourself. The white corpuscle count is back to normal." She reached an arm under his shoulders to help him check the panel behind him. He still looked pained.

"Tell me, Doctor," Kirk wanted to know. "Why are cures so often as painful as the disease?"

"Jim, that is a very sore subject with medical men."

"Dr. McCoy," Spock said reprovingly, "it seems that the Fabrini cure for granulation of the hemoglobin has seriously damaged your gift for witty repartee."

Nurse Chapel had filled the hypo again. "This is the last one, Doctor."

Spock, his eyes on the life support panel, achieved a Vulcan triumph. Joy radiated from his impassive face. "Your hemoglobin count is now completely normal, Doctor. So the flow of oxygen to all the cells of your body is again up to its abundantly energetic level."

McCoy sat up. "Spock, I owe this to you. Had you not brought back that Fabrini knowledge . . ."

"My translation abilities are one of my most minor accomplishments," Spock said. "If you consider my major ones, Doctor . . ."

"I wonder if there's a Fabrini cure for a swelled head," McCoy speculated.

Kirk intervened. "Bones, the Fabrini descendants are scheduled to debark on their promised planet in exactly fourteen months and seven days."

The grin left McCoy's face. He looked at Kirk.

"Yes," Kirk said. "I expect you'd like to see the Fabrini descendants again to thank them personally. So I've arranged to be in the vicinity of their new home at the time of their arrival. You will want to be there to welcome them, won't you?"

"Thank you, Jim," McCoy said. "Thank you very much."

PSYCHIC WORLD

Here are some of the leading books that delve into the world of the occult—that shed light on the powers of prophecy, of reincarnation and of foretelling the future.

☐ THE SEARCH FOR THE GIRL WITH THE BLUE EYES by Jess Stearn. The story of a young woman's reincarnation. (N4591—95¢)

☐ PSYCHIC PEOPLE by Eleanor Touhey Smith. The revealing account of 19 men and women with strange and supernatural powers. (N4471—95¢)

☐ EDGAR CAYCE: THE SLEEPING PROPHET by Jess Stearn. The bestselling study of the late mystic's prophecies and astounding readings. (Q6764—$1.25)

☐ A GIFT OF PROPHECY by Ruth Montgomery. The phenomenal account of Jeane Dixon's uncanny ability to forsee the future. (N4223—95¢)

☐ YOGA, YOUTH AND REINCARNATION by Jess Stearn describes the skeptical author's experience with the ancient art of yoga. (Q6508—$1.25)

☐ THE COMPLETE BOOK OF PALMISTRY by Joyce Wilson. A step-by-step fully-illustrated course in the ancient art of reading palms. (P5689—$1.00)

☐ PSYCHIC DISCOVERIES BEHIND THE IRON CURTAIN by Sheila Ostrander & Lynn Schroeder. Reports of government sponsored research on artificial reincarnation, astrological birth control and other psychic phenomena. Fully documented discoveries. (Q6581—$1.25)